Reluctant Client

Book 1 of Guardians, Inc. Series

L.B. Brookes

Contents

Dedication

For my husband- Brian- Thank you for encouraging and helping me to realize my dream.

For my family- Your encouragement and support mean the world to me.

Acknowledgment

Kathy- *Your help was what got me up and running!*

About the Author

L.B. Brookes is a new author writing contemporary romance novels that read more like an adventure movie. There is an exciting element about falling in love and she is eager to let readers experience this again and again alongside of her many new characters she creates for her stories. She is grateful for the little life nudges, that God has put in her path, so that it may lead to realizing her writing ambition and allowing it to grow.

When LB. Brookes is not writing, she is sailing with her husband and family on the Chesapeake Bay When that isn't possible she enjoys decorating her home, reading a good book, doting on her cat, and enjoying a walk with her family.

L.B. Brookes enjoys hearing from her readers, so please send her an email at lbb@lbbrookes.com

PROLOGUE

A zigzag burst of lightning streaked across the dark-grey sky, giving brief moments of illumination beyond his vehicle's high beams. As the boom of thunder followed the formidable light show a few seconds later, he came to a stop at the intersection.

Up ahead, the red traffic light rapidly blinked out a warning. Cautious of any oncoming movement, MJ turned onto Main Street, where the small town of Fairfax existed within several subsequential blocks.

No illuminated signs of business openings or the warming glow of the antiquated street lamps at each corner combated the darkness. Only candles and lanterns flickering through the roadside windows indicated the residents muddling through.

Soft whistling began harmonizing when one of his favorite classic rock songs came on the radio. His finger pressed the toggle control to increase the volume. In MJ's opinion, no one did 'Lucy in the Sky with Diamonds' quite like the Beatles. And it only made it more meaningful–reminding him of home–since he was so far from there on this stormy night.

Plus, MJ learned long ago to keep those pockets of his past alive and well. If not, one could get lost, and he refused to allow that to happen.

His attention briefly pulled away from his music to the weather's debris. Mother Nature's scattering mess resembled a war zone, except all the buildings looked intact.

Or mostly intact. A skimming glance off the road revealed a few property casualties.

Some broken windows and damaged roofs would require attention once everything calmed down. And those battered tree limbs–failing to bend to the strong winds–laid torn and splintered on the ground in the most inconvenient locations.

He maneuvered around them and other obstacles that discouraged full road access.

These back-to-back, violent storms had wreaked havoc on power lines throughout the east coast into the late night, and here outside of Washington, DC, was no exception.

This, combined with the earlier frequent stops to pull over for emergency and utility vehicles with their flashing lights, had prevented any increased speed.

It made getting to the established meeting place difficult but not impossible.

Another news update cycled through, and he lowered the radio's volume. It played in the background, competing with the lingering storm's rolling thunder, falling rain, and the steady beat of windshield wipers.

"Yeah, yeah," he muttered, sick of them cutting into his music.

All the local channels kept repeating themselves, predicting more power losses in the next few days. MJ leaned forward and gave a glance up toward the flashing sky. "Not that any of it will matter," he sighed.

There would be no excuses for being late due to bad weather, and apologizing should never be an option with these new associates. Plus, their taste in music was telling. MJ never understood when one's genre remained fixed to a singular style. What was wrong with having variety?

Slowing down again, MJ turned into a newly developed high-end business park. Rumors hinted that this was the future off-site headquarters of the FBI's new special division. He couldn't help but admire the set of balls it took to arrange this meeting place.

A high-pitched humming filled his cab's interior when lowering the tinted, bulletproof windows of his new Chevy Tahoe.

Pulling alongside the keypad terminal, he leaned outward and inhaled a deep breath. The cooling temperature and dampness of the night air were a welcoming change to the heated conditions inside. And he took the small break in the downpour as a good sign while tapping in the security code. The electronic notes of the punch key device almost sounded musical as they resonated in the stillness around him.

And a smirk moved across his mouth. *No power problems here.*

The state-of-the-art automatic gate quietly rolled open, and he drove through. His gaze went to the digital display on the dashboard. Despite all the delays, he was still a few minutes early, as usual.

Because MJ hated being late.

After all, 'Time means money' was Miles Jennings' mantra. One that had served him well over the years.

The Sons of Liberty shared that mantra but had one of their own too. Mistakes cost time and money. And knowing that either became irreplaceable once it was gone, this group took care of the spending of both.

Two mistakes occurred in these past weeks, and MJ realized the dire consequences of not being useful to these associates even if the reasons behind them served another purpose. "Let's just say time and money will no longer be a concern," he said, and his grip tightened on the steering wheel.

Even his music failed to soothe him.

But maybe that was best. Distractions were unwise now that he drew nearer.

He shifted in his seat and looked around, noting the secured construction perimeter with an impenetrable security fence. It would be wise to be concerned, and MJ could definitely be called sensible, as well as ambitious and resourceful.

After all, getting to this level within the organization had not been an easy feat. And since the plan was to continually rise higher, that meant serious damage control tonight. "I'll figure something out." He rolled his shoulders as an expression of dire purpose reflected back in the rear-view mirror.

The light-grey Bentley Mulsanne parked up ahead had its motor running. Two dark construction trailers stood side by side–like sentinels–just behind the parked car. Low illumination concealed the surrounding area, making it a good place for dark deeds.

With the other car's tinted windows, it became anyone's guess on how many were attending tonight's meeting.

Easing behind the waiting car, MJ parked and switched off the vehicle's motor.

The Bentley's driver door promptly swung open. A man in a grey-colored uniform stepped out. MJ remained seated and watched as the chauffeur opened the back passenger's door with a smooth competence. As if he matched the movements to an inner song playing in his head. MJ suspected something classical, like Winter of Vivaldi's Four Seasons, represented that one's personality well.

Schooling his features to remain neutral became difficult. That man, Michael Arenald, with his uppity attitude, continued to get on MJ's last nerve. He let the clenched fists of both hands relax and shook his head. Allowing those thoughts to reign over him would do no good.

When the chauffeur moved away to provide a discreet separation from the man now exiting the car, MJ took his cue, jumped out of his vehicle, and walked toward the contact.

On the newly formed concrete curb, a man stood waiting.

By his outward appearance, he looked like an opera lover. The formal attire of the white tailored shirt and impeccable bow tie contrasted sharply with the glossy black tuxedo jacket and matching slacks. Stealing a glimpse down at his off-the-rack business suit, MJ wondered if it appeared utterly inappropriate in comparison.

But his smile gleamed with confidence, nonetheless, as he greeted his boss. Reaching out to shake hands, he called out, "Good evening, Mr. Black. I hope you've had no difficulties with the roads tonight."

The man ignored the outstretched hand, instead adjusting the cuffs on his pristine tailored jacket. Only after completing this task did he look up to meet MJ's guarded expression.

"I don't have difficulties, Jennings-"

"Call me MJ-"

"Jennings." The quiet yet clipped tone reflected his dislike for the interruption. "If I become aware of concerns or difficulties, well… the employee is no longer the best and will no longer be of use to me." He shifted to address his chauffeur. "Is this not so, Michael?"

"That is correct, Sir." He bowed slightly in respect. His voice held a refined quality to it, with a strong posh accent.

The distinguished gentleman turned away from the chauffeur to address one of many underlings within the organization. "I had assumed that the little matter we discussed at our last meeting would be completed."

MJ cleared his throat before replying, "I did meet with some resistance. However, recent steps in place will secure success in the upcoming weeks. You will not be disappointed. Not only will the task be completed very soon, but I have set in place a tool that may have other uses for us in the future." In his smooth tone, he clearly relayed his certainty.

His mentor nodded slowly in thoughtful reflection. "Yes. I read your report. I can see where you might believe that is true. Although now, it will be much harder to complete without exposing others already in place." His voice got intensely quiet. "This issue needed results promptly."

"Well… Yes. I understand. But I want to explain in detail my recent endeavors that will rectify this slight delay immediately."

MJ's voice stayed clear and strong. His smile remained confident.

Mr. Black pivoted on the sole of his shoes and began walking back toward the car. The chauffeur glided forward in synchronized timing, ready to hold the door open for him. A short, inaudible murmuring transpired between Mr. Black and his chauffeur before he disappeared into the car's interior.

Michael, the very efficient driver–or anything else the organization required–shut the door silently and moved to stand before MJ. "Regrettably, your services are no longer required."

Unaware of the gun and too late to do anything about it, MJ's body jerked with the two shots fired. The silencer on the weapon concealed most of the sound, eliminating any concern or curiosity in the neighboring area. The bullets passed through his lower abdomen and became lodged in the construction trailer behind MJ's collapsed body.

Back inside the dimness of the Bentley's interior, a cough broke the silence. "What do you want me to do with this?" Mr. Edward Sharpe sat in the plush sedan's interior, facing his new immediate supervisor.

"Make it go away," Mr. Black directed. "Take the lead. Make the adjustments we talked about." Sharpe reached for the door handle and let himself out, pausing when his employer added,

"Keep the Tahoe. But do not... alter my directives as Mr. Jennings did."

Sharpe headed for the trailer to dig out the evidence embedded in the exterior wall. He went around the building and got the other supplies needed for this errand. "Black's shadow certainly thought of everything," Sharpe muttered, pushing aside the heavier items to get to the folded tarp. His gaze went back to his new car.

A sweet ride indeed and no reason to get it dirty so soon.

Another glance toward the street showed the car and the elite organization's third in command long gone. Their lofty ambitions of world dominance had no time for cleaning up messes.

That's why a man like him would always be needed.

With careful steps, Sharpe made his way back to the curb. Two bullet shells got picked up and placed in his coat's pocket as he went to spread out the brown, waterproof material next to the reposed body.

Groaning nearby, MJ knew that calculated design and not poor shooting provided the present results of his wounds' location.

His death was meant to take some time.

Chapter One

Good morning, JSB3." The female answering the phone sounded out of breath but in pleasant humor for an early, rainy Wednesday morning.

William J. Maxwell IV blew out a short burst of air. "Morning, Debbie. It's Will."

A slight pause preceded an agitated reply, "I know who it is." Her guarded silence followed.

"I need to speak to you about Allison," Will explained. Another disgruntled sigh sounded loud and clear in his ear. Since there had been a fifty-fifty chance of another person answering instead, he wanted to do the same. His head began banging like a marching band on steroids.

Because the odds had worked against him, it seemed only fitting this call would obliterate the good mood of the one who did pick up. Though, to be fair, she wouldn't label it a win either by taking his call.

"We can't keep doing this. I don't want her to leave to avoid the awkward situation."

Debbie's statement of Allison's reaction was no bluff. If it ever came out that he kept tabs on her whereabouts over the years, it wouldn't go well.

"Hell," he muttered under his breath. Knowing if Allison ever found out about his connection with her uncle, she would go nuclear on his ass.

The reasons this time were legitimate. Although he doubted that would make any difference with her cooperation.

Will shook his head as those other previous times came to mind. To claim the same would be a lie, and because of it, his worry circled over and over in his mind.

Was he to blame?

He rifled through the papers on the desk and pulled the old newspaper article out in front. The bold, black lettering headline read: **Buchanan Patriarch dies in a fiery crash**.

Several articles, coming out because of recent events, recirculated the old mysterious circumstances surrounding her father's car accident for the sole purpose of selling newspapers. Will had to hand it to them: **Buchanan Curse strikes again**, was a snappy catchphrase.

Allison believed that the family's misfortunes laid solely on this Buchanan's curse, but Will put no creditable bearing on any of that nonsense.

Still, the gossip rags weren't that far off from the truth. And Allison losing her mom and stepfather in a private plane crash years later, came up in the stories too. Reminding readers that with no significant leads to follow and nothing solved about their deaths, Allison had become a very wealthy heiress at the young age of twelve.

"I take it that she's not there right now," Will confirmed. His one hand reached up as his eyelids lowered. The quick massage with his thumb and forefinger helped distribute the lack of moisture within his dry eyes.

"Yes. But I expect her in at any minute," Debbie snapped at him.

Before making this call, Will had reviewed the schedule in an open file on his desk. His watch-like device currently showed military time. The display reverted to standard time when pressing a small button, indicating the early morning hour.

"I should go." Debbie's gaze darted to the front entrance.

"It can't be helped," Will explained.

Because of those tragedies murked in shadows and the disastrous short marriage before meeting Will, Allison would cut ties–real quick–if things didn't remain crystal clear. And be inclined to take issue with others' actions inferring with her perceived freedom.

Plus, she had enough resources to make finding her whereabouts difficult.

Not impossible for Will to find, but still time-consuming, and they didn't have time to spare. Even if Allison wasn't aware of it.

Yet.

"Stop putting me in the middle!" Her heavy volume rang in Will's ears, causing him to wince. Loyalty meant everything to Debbie. Even to those she had held grudges against for years.

Those such as Will.

He blew out a silent exhale of air. He barked, having no time for arguing and going down that particular rabbit hole, "Meet me at Jim's around 1:30."

A colossal regret surfaced of ever disclosing that restaurant to Will. With the exterior facade resembling a dive bar and only a slight improvement to its interiors, the establishment looked like something to avoid at all costs. But the surprisingly good food and drinks made it a locals' well-guarded secret.

One that she would be careful ever to share again.

Debbie's history with Will allowed her to recognize his tone. Arguing would serve no purpose. "Fine," she reluctantly agreed but fiercely added, "You're buying!"

"Oh, and Debbie..." Will paused to assure she was still on the line.

"What?" she added with a loud huff. An open palm smacked the desk surface.

He laughed despite the serious circumstances. "She'll be taking more than a few weeks off very shortly. You might want to start looking at your options. Gotta go. Don't be late."

"Wait... What?"

When hearing the dial tone, the phone got set back on its cradle very slowly. "Shit," Debbie mumbled while blankly staring ahead. Her thoughts raced a mile a minute.

A hand lightly squeezed her shoulder.

She looked up at her husband, Jake, and released a pent-up breath in slow increments. "Something's up." Shifting further in her seat, Debbie met her husband's deep blue gaze and added, "I think he knows."

"It would be hard for him not to catch wind of it. They certainly gave it enough coverage." Jake's eyebrow went up high on the forehead, getting lost behind his long bangs as he leaned further down.

Debbie reached over to tuck those dark-brown locks behind his ears that desperately needed a haircut. She shrugged. "He kept the conversation short, sweet, and one-sided, as usual." Her frowning facial expression, paired with the sarcasm in her response, clearly showed her feelings on the matter. She rested an elbow on the desk and leaned her forehead down onto an open hand. Her hand began massaging away the beginnings of a tension headache.

"You know he's supposed to be our friend, too," Jake softly inserted.

"I know that! I can still be pissed at him, can't I?"

"Three years is a long time to still be angry."

"Well, remember that if you ever decide to cheat on me as he did on Allison. But, in your case, I will draw blood," Debbie vowed.

"Love… I see no one but you." Jake's expression gentled while looking into his wife's dark-brown eyes swirling with deep emotions. This fiercely loyal nature was one of the many things he admired about his wife. Only a selected few got within the inner circle. However difficult to obtain, Jake grinned, knowing she made it worth one's while in his case.

Tugging on the loose corkscrew strand of her light-brown hair that reminded him of warm melted caramel–Jake's favorite sweet tooth treat–he pulled with a soft touch. "We must stay out of whatever is between him and Allison."

"Well… maybe you're-"

A buzzing of their entrance door interrupted her. Her swift look to Jake passed along a silent message with a fleeting expression. One which her husband easily understood.

This conversation would continue later.

When the storefront entryway opened, a heavy whip of wind and rain preceded a very determined petite woman through the threshold. This new arrival laughed while trying to win a struggle with the wind, an opened umbrella, and a heavy door. All while trying to keep a hold of numerous items in her grasp.

Although the wind held the advantage in this scrimmage, unencumbered with caring about anything other than which direction to blow, the young woman gave it her all. And thanks to fashioning her thick, wavy masses of dark chestnut hair into a coiffed twist today, she wasn't fighting with those long locks blocking her vision on top of everything else.

For a brief moment, the bright-red umbrella blocked her classical, aristocratic features held on a slim, oval-shaped face. But with less-than-smooth maneuvering, she managed to get inside with everything still in her possession. A victory laugh had the last say as the doorway shut and the wind went on its blustery way. "Hey! We have power!" The easygoing, cheerful voice contradicted the polished, crisp appearance of wearing the latest Versace dark, pink-colored, rain jacket and black Gucci pumps.

Her hazel eyes flashed bright with humor, putting the dreary rainy day to shame in comparison. "I got bagels and cream cheese. And boy was that an accomplishment." Allison quickly juggled the abundant assortment of decorating items held in each arm. A large, cumbersome bag slid off the right shoulder onto the nearest desk.

The very same one Jake and Debbie presently occupied.

Jake reached for the bag. The aroma of Jake's favorite sesame seed bagels made his mouth water.

Allison pulled the fancy, recycled paper bag further away. "Ah ahh," the young woman teased. Her lips—wide, full, and naturally pink—always looked for an excuse to smile. As she mischievously did with Jake and Debbie before disclosing, "There are strings attached. You have to help me get all the stuff I took out yesterday back onto their shelves." The bartering contents got dangled and shook in her grasp. Their tantalizing smells of toasted bready goodness swirled more profoundly around them.

She plopped another canvas bag onto the floor and leaned a hip on the desk. "I swear my right arm is longer than my left with all the samples I carry out of here daily."

While scooping up that previously discarded tote from the floor, Allison continued talking about yesterday's meeting with a new client and how promising that contract looked. And that same abused bag got dumped with a dramatic flair onto the front entrance's conference tabletop before she headed toward the exit.

Only then did the realization hit. Allison's eyes–squinting to a narrowing focus–landed on the company's owners, who gave no greetings or responses back to what she had been discussing.

It didn't go amiss either that those two were looking at her rather strangely.

After all, still being very much in love, they were not afraid of public displays of affection. Their six years of marriage and working together often came with those two blurring the lines between their appropriate private and business boundaries.

And a whole lot more.

A quick shudder passed along Allison's body when a particular instance came to mind. "No one should be that flexible," she muttered.

Shaking off that unwanted visual memory, Allison's loud exhale preceded her, calling out, "Come on, guys! Snap out of it. I'm gone for meetings most of this week, and then you will be left to your own devices for the next two weeks." A quick shimmy dance in place accompanied the information. "Vacation, here I come! By the time I get back, Deb, I'll be able to compete with you and all your coco-licious coloring."

Looking back over the shoulder, she sent them a teasing look. "You can..." Allison's lips pressed together, holding in a snort before adding, "Continue whatever, then. Right now, get your butts in gear!"

She smirked again when their expressions both froze in guilt. With her earlier suspicion reinforced, Allison snatched up her umbrella left by the door. Laughter trickled out behind her and got swept up in the swirling winds as she exited the building.

A few seconds passed before Debbie and Jake locked gazes and then shrugged. But as they started to follow Allison, Debbie's light grasp on her husband's arm delayed them. She tilted her head toward the entrance. "We'll find out what he... wants. And then agree on what to tell her."

"Deal," Jake agreed. "How did she know... we? Um-" His eyebrows wiggled up and down.

"Ah, never mind." He quickly placed two fingers against his wife's lips staying any further comments. From her fire-cracker, glittering eyes, he wanted to remain clueless, knowing full well that women shared the damnedest things when wine was involved. "I hope she remembered I like the salmon cream spread. It's fantastic."

Suddenly an umbrella got shoved into his ribs. "Ouch!" Jake shot his wife a wounded look.

Debbie's push prompted him out the door faster before he hastily sidestepped away from her reach.

"Hey, wait! Don't pick that up. It looks heavy!" Jake shouted when spotting Allison attempting to lift a large box while the wind threatened to scoop up her umbrella. "Let Debbie help you with that." He shot a cheeky wink to his wife.

Shaking her head, Debbie pushed him out of the way with an exasperated groan. But while heading over to help her friend, the seriousness of Will's call divided her focus. A gut feeling wouldn't go away. Something brewed murky around them. And a storm gathered at their doors that had nothing to do with the weather. She and Jake would be there for Allison without a doubt.

But deep down, Debbie knew Will Maxwell was better suited for troubled times.

After all, he was the one with the superhero powers.

Chapter Two

The following day, two of Will Maxwell's best agents secured the surrounding area where he was about to meet with Jake, Debbie, and Allison.

Will paced the cobblestone driveway that stood before the garage's double doors. With a gun in his right hand pointed toward the ground, he reached into his back pocket with the other and pulled out a cell phone.

With his thumb skimming the display's surface, the company's patented security program unlocked the device. A quick touch on the icon button on the screen had a speed dial number going through. The call got picked up immediately.

"What the hell happened?" a harsh, barking voice asked.

Will pulled the phone slightly away from the ear but angled the microphone area near his mouth. "Someone activated the alarm on the security panel where I'll be meeting..." He flipped over his wrist to view a unique watch before continuing, "In fifteen minutes. If I know Allison, she'll be a few minutes early."

"Do you want to bail?"

"No! We're doing this. She's already en route. Two teams are shadowing. I'll make sure the premises are secured. What's your ETA?"

"Five minutes," the caller promised.

A snap of a stick had Will spinning around.

Two intruders, covered from head to toe in camo gear, came around the side yard's landscaping perimeter. With their weapons pointed at Will.

These men weren't Guardians, Inc. employees.

With a gun up in seconds, aiming at center mass, Will's shot rang true. And one of the two infiltrators fell to the ground.

The other man continued to advance even when Will's gunfire was aimed directly at him.

But the bullets just bounced off an invisible shield.

Shit!

Possible options raced through his mind. *Could be just a shield or telekinesis.* But when the trespasser didn't follow through with any kinetic energy to take Will down, it narrowed the options to one.

He's a shield.

With swift movements, his cell phone got tossed to the ground in a nearby pile of leaves. The sounds of shouting could still be heard spilling out from the device in a muffled murmur. Hoping backup would arrive soon, Will engaged the lock on the gun and threw the weapon close to the discarded phone.

One hand reached out toward the garage wall's exterior face–specifically to the exterior outlet. The outlet's cover exploded away into charred bits with a loud pop. A bolt of electricity shot out, making a beeline to Will's outstretched hand. His wrist-device served more as a custom-paired, cell-biomechanics and electrical-impulsion mini-computer than just a timepiece. With these specialized features, it defused the pulsing energy, diverted it back to its host, and contained some of the electrical charges within a storage chamber.

Swinging out with one leg extended back, Will's other leg became slightly bent to crouch forward and provide stability.

A blast of streaming energy resembling lightning headed toward the advancing opponent. With this release of power, a surge of euphoric adrenaline hit like a drug coursing in Will's veins.

The stranger's shield took the initial hit. But Will's power would prove significantly stronger. His steady flow of electricity began weakening the other man's protective covering.

A rush of heavy footsteps came from around the front of the house.

For just a split second, a glance to the side revealed one of the Guardians, Inc. men pursuing another intruder, causing Will's effort to get divided. He stepped backward, closer to the nearby exterior wall.

Although looking away for only a short moment, it allowed the 'shielding' opponent to dart between a few trees.

The electrical attack immediately cut off, and Will swore under his breath.

There was no random explanation possible that could easily explain the loss of so many trees to the realty company. Let alone someone with his exceptional abilities did the damage.

"Fuck, fuck!" Will muttered, watching as the interloper took off through the wooded grouping. His focus returned to his men just in time to spot the other intruder racing to the neighbor's driveway across the street.

Will sprinted to the pile of leaves, skidding across the cobblestone pavers to slam knees down on the ground. Searching, he used the loud cursing voice coming out from the phone as a guide.

When fingers brushed up against a cold, flat surface, he grabbed the phone and rested it against the ear. "Jeff-"

"What the blue blazes! I'm pulling in-"

A rubber skid on asphalt had Will's concentration drawn to the street below.

The neighbor's car came barreling out of the garage across the way. With debris thrown outward in destructive disarray, a vehicle headed to the stretch of lawn between the property next door.

Will cursed again as the SUV slipped and slid through the trees, steering in a wide bank and heading further up the road. To only have taken a sudden, sharp bootleg's turn. Reversing the direction of travel at 180 degrees, the car came to a screeching stop at the opposite side of the road.

A man bolted out from the tree line. The same foe that had gotten away from Will jumped into the vehicle on the passenger's side. The soccer-mom's getaway car took off and left the residential development.

Jeff's vehicle turned onto the same road the intruders were fleeing down. Yelling into the cell phone, Will ordered, "White. Buick. Enclave. Get it!"

The Guardians Inc.'s agents jogged up to Will. "You okay, boss?" one of them asked.

A frown marred Will's features as he spared them a darting glance. His nod served as an affirmative reply before he swiftly angled back to the development's entryway. Both vehicles were long gone.

"Jeff's got 'em," he said while shifting back around. "Go, make sure no one else is around, secure things, and then go across the way. Handle the police. I don't know how they found us..." Will reached into the mulch again and found his gun. He secured it in his side harness and stood up. Bringing his scrutiny back to the security team, he said with a tone–that clued them all in–that he wasn't a person to mess with right now.

"Our client is on the way. I want her to stay safe."

****

Allison found herself rushed to an unexpected meeting scheduled by Jake and Debbie located on the outskirts of Philadelphia in a town called Chadds Ford. Looking down again at the hand-drawn directions Jake gave her, she scowled while shaking the paper. The urge to chuck it out the window became overwhelming.

She was lost–yet again.

And Allison hated being lost. And late.

Where and when. With fortitude and planning, one could be tricked into thinking that the chaos of life could be manageable. But when reality messed with the illusion, things often got messy.

Holding on tight to false hope curbed the panic about compromising both categories. "My destination is probably right around the next corner," she insisted, using her best-selling tone–the one used for presenting her interior vision to a client.

"Yeah, right!" she snorted. The delusional bubble popped as her voice carried loudly across the top 40's music on Satellite Radio.

She grumbled loudly, "Debbie probably gave Jake these darn directions."

The visual cue of the old train station turned pub indicated the small side road she needed to be on. A quick jerk on the steering wheel had the car swerving left. According to the directions, tightly gripped in her hand, it was supposed to be on the right.

Aggravated thoughts on her friend's directional skills were interrupted by the blare of a car horn from behind. An absent-minded wave apologized to the nearby driver. Even the precaution of leaving early this morning wasn't enough compensation for following Jake's directions. However, Allison would bet her trust fund that this was the work of DDD, Directional-Dysfunctional-Debbie.

After two more misdirection's where numerous agitated drivers showed their feelings through hand gestures and blaring horns, Allison sagged in relief to finally find the house. But glancing at the dashboard's digital clock made her slip out, "Shit!"

An immediate cringe before a chided whisper, "Watch your mouth," soon followed afterward. Knowing that once she headed down that potty-mouth path, it became much harder to curb those impulses.

Flashing lights from a police car parked along the two-lane street took attention away from the road. She could make out the damage to the neighbor's garage door before turning into the driveway across the way. A grimace stole across her face.

"I've had my share of parking mishaps," she uttered under her breath in sympathy.

The long winding driveway showed a scattering of unfinished plantings and recently started garden projects along the property's landscape. Spring fever took hold for a brief moment. A wistful sigh burst from her lips as she parked. And a longing to do their outdoor projects instead of their interior ones settled upon a weary heart.

A vacation couldn't come soon enough. Keeping up the pretense was exhausting.

Her attention remained distracted as she jumped out and faced the side panel. Clicking the button on the key remote, the door slid open. "One good thing about minivans is the magic genie door opener," she joked while leaning inside into the back seats.

"Well... since that's the only good thing, and Hell... hasn't frozen over. Why are you driving one? "

Chapter Three

The sound of that male's voice coming out of nowhere made Allison stumble forward into the back seat. And the rest of her good mood fell just as quickly.

To make matters worse, her derriere became effectively displayed in this precarious predicament. She wanted to groan at the unfairness of it all. Even permitting herself a mini-meltdown seemed like a good thing to do. But she took a deep cleansing pull of air into her lungs and left those childish—not to mention unproductive—ways of dealing with adversity in her past.

Instead, she gathered the portfolio cases and other designer tools before straightening back up. She would remain professional, even if it killed her.

Her lungs stilled while her mind frantically raced. The limited options became clear. Should she face him or allow the equally unsettling choice of having his eyes remain on her like a physical caress?

Either way proved problematic.

Besides, climbing in and heading toward the driver's seat appeared even more difficult. So, puffing out a large exhale, she mentally shored up her defenses and pivoted around.

His quick grin and devilish sparkling eyes confirmed her suspicions.

Damn him! A curse popped out silently.

William Maxwell often got called a computer geek. But he stood before Allison with all of the physical characteristics of an avid outdoorsman. With tall, broad shoulders narrowed down to a trim, fit waist, toned abdominal area, and well-defined arms, he reinforced an abundant vitality through an incredible physique.

Even while wearing a battered National Park sweatshirt and his dark, almost black-colored hair falling disheveled around his face, could anyone deny the outcome? Or could the sight of well-worn-in jeans smeared with dirt marks on each knee take away the impact of seeing him again?

No, they could not. He still looked fantastic.

Is it too much to ask that he gain weight... ten pounds or so? No doubt, that wishful thought escaped, and never did there stand a more impossible outcome.

Will would never slow down enough to let that happen.

Yes, spending time behind a computer and in meetings filled most of the Guardians, Inc's CEO's workday when they were a couple. But traveling for clients, checking in on multiple site locations, and training also filled his days, not to mention the imagery that quickly popped into Allison's mind of all those hours he spent in the gym.

With movements reflecting a steady, determined rhythm and often a single-minded purpose, Will's demeanor shouted dangerous. Deadly.

And the hand-to-hand know-how and weapons training–although impressive–didn't cover his full arsenal of talents.

What made William Maxwell so threatening came from his intelligence. Like the mind of a supercomputer, he could process information quickly, retain a long memory, and have an annoying preference for logical decisions.

Those decisions usually became counterpoints to most of her own. And proved to kick up heated debates between them.

So, while Allison thoroughly checked him out and reminisced about those passionate discussions, Will looked to be doing the same. His grin flashed to a full-fledged smile. Amusement caused the golden specks in his brown eyes to twinkle brightly.

"It's rude to do that, you know," she hissed, knowing he was probably reading her mind.

Because above all else, the Guardians, Inc.'s owner had the added advantage of being among an elite group of people who had access to the unknown regions of the mind.

And because Will didn't talk much about these unique gifts, Allison didn't know which became the stronger of the two. Either the power that allowed the manipulation of electricity and electronic devices or the mind-reading ability could be the winning ticket.

Both physical and mental attributes served him well as a successful executive in his privately-owned company. However, the extra abilities kept him in high demand as a consultant for the Federal Bureau of Investigations and other similar agencies. Although, only a few knew about how Will really accessed his information.

"What are you doing here?" Allison observed the scuff marks and the rips around the knees.

"I'm working security for the homeowner," Will casually explained.

Taking a step away, she dismissed him and what she thought of his stupid smile. She clicked the door closed and marched toward the front walkway. "Can't afford a decent pair of jeans, I see. I thought owning your own company paid well." She remarked, knowing full well that he had been loaded even before his company took off as it did.

"It's good to see you too." Will laughed. "We can use the side entrance." He casually rested a hand in the middle of her back, guiding her in the opposite direction toward the back patio.

She allowed his touch only until spotting the other path. "Ah, thanks." Unable to handle even that brief connection. "I think I can see myself to the door. You can do-" She hastily skipped ahead. "Whatever it is that you were doing." A hand airily gestured. She was eager to have him on his way.

"That's ok." His long stride gained ground quickly. "I was coming this way when you pulled up." They reached the side patio's entrance together. Will leaned in, and an arm brushed against her left breast as he tugged the sliding glass door open.

You did that on purpose. You big fat Jerk. Allison pushed her thoughts toward him. Her eyes glittered with shards of icy disdain, and her smile became equally chilling. "Thanks, I can manage from here."

"Never doubted it for a minute." A devilish smile flashed back, and knowing she couldn't read his mind as he could hers, teasingly added, "You wish."

He pointed to a casual sitting area that took full advantage of the natural sunlight pouring in. "Why don't you set those things down over there?" He spotted the brief hesitation before she proceeded further into the room.

A large circular coffee table dominated the sunroom. Too unnerved by her ex-lover's presence, any care for causing damage flew out the window. All the fabric and wallpaper books, paint samples, and portfolios of past projects got dropped on top. She plopped onto the adjacent sofa, facing a brick fireplace, and casually sorted through her things.

Never expecting a reunion quite like this, Allison's pulse was going a mile-a-minute. *Sara!* Became instantly followed by another panicked thought. *Okay, I can't think about that-*

With the preoccupation of unpacking and keeping her thoughts locked down, Allison remained unaware of the effects that her present location provided. The sunlight spilled all around her, adding a sheen to her skin, catching her auburn hair, and creating a prism-like halo behind her.

Will couldn't stop the fanciful notion of her glowing with magic. But it did get quickly pushed from his mind. He cleared his throat and said, "Can I get anything for you?" Spotting the tilting of Allison's head accompanied by a bewildered expression, he added, "Something to drink?"

"Oh, no thanks," she said softly. A brief pause occurred before she added in a rush, "Do you have more than just a business connection to the owner?"

Will could have set his watch on a three-second buzzer for what happened next. The nodding of his head–indicating yes– had her facial expression change and the release of the timer set.

One. Two. Bzzz.

"Oh, God! Don't tell me she's one in a long line of parading girlfriends," she hissed. "I... I don't care how much she is willing to pay. Or... you, for that matter!" She began gathering her things to make a hasty retreat.

Will bounced up to block her. "Allison, that is not what is going on here."

She tried to get around him, but with each sequential attempt, he intercepted, cajoling her into hearing him out.

A warm and fuzzy personality definitely wouldn't describe Will. Even on a good day, it became hard for most people to take him in small doses before his abrupt mannerisms would push them further off guard. So, after numerous attempts to be good, his minuscule amount of patience finally ran out.

"Will. You. Stop. For one Goddamn minute!" He took her hands into one of his, halting her latest attempt to gather as much stuff as possible.

Allison tugged on her hands and glared at him when they remained imprisoned.

"Calm the fuck down!" He took a deep breath and tried for a more reassuring demeanor. "Let me get us something to drink, and then I can expla-"

"If you think I'm staying to hear anything YOU have to say... Think again, Big Shot FBI consultant!" A precise, hard kick to his shin got her hands released. Reaching back for her purse among all the other items, she huffed out, "Keep everything else!"

Her hand had just pried the sliding door open to leave when the frantic ringing of a doorbell started in the distance.

"Oh, now they get here!" In frustration, Will threw up his hands before rushing out of the room in the opposite direction.

And this preoccupation gave Allison an excellent opportunity to get the Hell out of Dodge. She moved as rapidly as her throbbing foot would allow, muttering the whole way back to the van.

But an added complication halted her progress. Someone's car had successfully blocked the exit.

"Damn it!" She stomped her foot on the cobblestone driveway, wincing in pain immediately afterward.

The sound of fast-approaching footsteps had her spinning around. She wasted no time scowling at the pair of soon-to-be ex-friends, who both carried pitifully sorry-looking expressions all over their faces. With hands on her hips and one foot tapping the ground, Allison waited for their approach.

"We had no choice," Debbie quickly tried to explain. "I wanted to get here before you, but-"

"But you got lost!" Allison finished.

Debbie tilted her head toward the sky and groaned.

Allison pivoted and pointed her finger at Jake. "I specifically asked you for directions!" There was no logical reason for her to fixate on the wrong directions. But she couldn't help it even though she had bigger fish to fry regarding their traitorous betrayal.

"I know. I know." Jake frowned and held his palms open, facing Allison in surrender. "You'd think I would learn by now. However, this time, I was under duress."

Catching the tail end of the conversation, Will followed up behind them, near Allison.

"I'm not cut out for this spy stuff, like some people." Jake directed that comment and all his annoyance at this unwanted situation at his lifelong friend.

"Well... Let's all go back inside and talk." Will ignored the dig while lightly resting a hand on the middle of Allison's back to guide her inside.

Allison stiffened and braced to remain unmovable.

Simultaneously, her gaze darted to Debbie, to their car, and then back to Debbie. The silent demand of raised eyebrows and the chin jerk toward the item blocking the exit became quite clear.

But instead of helping a friend out–both metaphorically and literally, Allison groaned in frustration as Debbie shook her head frantically back and forth.

Chapter Four

In an undisclosed location, several states away, Edward Sharpe's large frame–fitted in a custom-made suit from his New York City tailor–had just sat down. He shifted in the chair and rolled into position before the desk in his new office–for the first time.

And everything felt off-scaled. Small.

Inadequate for his body size–which still kept the beefy-trim frame from his underground street-fighting beginnings. And more importantly, it was deficient for his most recent elevated position. After all, he believed rewarding one's successes was just as necessary as punishing one's failures.

Edward recalled the last words uttered from Miles Jennings' lips before discarding his dying body in the New River's floodwaters. "Please... No!" the man had begged.

Two words–that held little to no meaning to Edward Sharpe. "I will not make the same dumbass mistakes as my predecessor," he said as a vow to himself, having every intention of following most of Black's orders.

However, some of those directives would get shifted to benefit Sharpe's agenda. "I just won't get caught," Edward smugly whispered.

Someone knocked on the office door and immediately walked in, disrupting his contemplations.

"Next time, wait until I tell you to come in," he uttered with deliberate patience. Demanding the respect due to him. Believing he deserved it for being a self-made man despite his humble origins.

"I'm very sorry, Sir, it won't happen again."

"See that it doesn't, with anyone else as well. It will not matter who your Aunt is. I will hold you accountable for their mistakes. Do I make myself clear?"

"Yes, Sir."

"Good. What is on the agenda today?"

With a slim and petite stature, the mousy-looking assistant stumbled briefly with her clipboard before responding. She began listing Sharpe's appointments, reading off from the printed schedule that would be shredded at the end of the day. "You have a meeting with Mr. Green and Mr. Black in twenty minutes concerning the FBI's informants. The report is on your desk."

"Speak up, woman! I can barely hear you." Sharpe tapped his fingers rapidly on top of the desk's surface. When she lost the grip on the items in her hands, he took pleasure in her apparent nervousness.

Her timid brown-colored eyes darted to Sharpe's cold, dark-blue irises before jumping to the slight bump on his crooked nose. She cleared her throat. And in a much louder voice, she said, "You have some flexibility with your 10:30 appointment. I notified the participants that the meeting might start late and run short. The car is ready for your 11:50 departure. Your driver understands that you must be notified immediately if any traffic considerations prevent you from making the lunch meeting at 12:30."

"That will be all, Daniels. Hold all my calls for this upcoming meeting and my lunch appointment." He dismissed his assistant to review the open file.

Relieved with this dismissal, she hurried toward the door.

"Oh, Daniels?" Edwards quietly spoke while keeping his head down, reading.

"Yes, Sir?" A stiffened pause preceded her turning back.

"You are aware that Mr. Black does not drink coffee?"

"I will provide his tea preference in the beverage choices when they arrive."

"One more thing. I want to review office furniture selections when I return from lunch."

"Understood, Sir, right away." Making her way out, she quietly shut the door. Her frame slowly lowered down to the office chair. A slow exhale was released as she stiffly settled herself before the computer.

The desk faced the closed door she had just exited. Typing in the code to reactivate the monitor screen, she efficiently searched for many furniture dealers in the area while waiting for the scheduled visitors to arrive. Her hand, bare of rings and other female adornments trembled before fumbling for the receiver.

****

Allison contently drifted in a pleasantly warm cocoon until a persistent tapping on the cheek prevented her from getting some much-deserved rest. A dream about sun-baked shores on a tropical island awaited her return. She wanted to be left alone to enjoy it.

"Come on, beautiful. Let me see those gorgeous eyes of yours."

Oh… Well, if that's the way it is. A hint of a smile appeared on Allison's face as that voice coaxed her from the current dream world into another, more tempting one.

"That's it. Come on, sweetheart."

Pouting, she moved her head. The press of a cheek into the pillow trapped his hand and stopped the tapping. When snuggling into that sturdy palm, a deep, resounding chuckle seeped into her fantasy. She knew that sexy chuckle.

One hand pushed through the heavy mist of dreams to reach up and cup the masculine contours of a cheek and chin. The other hand brushed softly, aiming to enjoy the texture of the thick, wavy hair. Sighing, Allison slowly opened her eyes.

"There they are," Will said, referring to Allison's eyes, their shape with thick, long, sweeping lashes held a touch of the exotic. A trait inherited from Sara Marie Buchanan, her mother. Allison's eye color could alter from a misty steel-grey to forest green, depending on the clothing worn or the lighting around her.

Today, her irises stayed more green than blue while staring back at him in sleepy reflection.

In their past relationship, getting Will to slow down for lazy mornings together became extremely difficult. So, like, then, when it did happen, she had savored those times. Her fingers traced the grooves on the face hovering before her.

The corner of Will's eyes held laugh lines, which Allison found ironic since he took everything upon his shoulders—so seriously.

Will took in her far-away expression. He, too, remembered those indulging snippets of time. And when thinking back to those incidents, they were not nearly as frequent enough.

So, having the advantage now, he did not hesitate.

Even expecting the consequences, he could not stop. Because of the intense attraction between them, resisting that pull became so much more complicated.

His mouth lowered to brush up against hers.

The luscious softness of her lips' rounded shape welcomed his invasion. But it didn't quench the need. He gathered her closer, wanting more. She smelled of freshly laundered cotton sheets and apple blossoms. Desire clouded his earlier focus as the kiss went deeper.

Craving the same thing, Allison reached around to hold him tighter. *Feels so good.* Allison soaked up the sensations, causing a chain reaction, running rampage through her system.

Will groaned when her hands wandered down to his chest, molding and pressing while trailing a path down his body.

When pulling the worn cotton fabric of his sweatshirt up, she got skin access. Allison felt his body shudder in response. She couldn't get enough of the warm, taut surface pulled over the contours of coiled muscles. This body held so much strength, and she became dizzy, knowing what her touch could do to him.

How come it feels so right with this man and no other? Her body arched into his embrace to get even closer.

But wakefulness began pressing to the surface.

Other... other... Those thoughts had the dream bubble burst. Her body instantaneously lost its compliance and became stiff in his embrace. Arms that had just held him tightly–now pushed him away.

Will eased back, letting his gaze travel, studying the nuances of the kiss still lingering on her face. Flushed cheeks from sleep, desire, and swollen lips now a deeper shade of pink due to her teeth biting down on the lower lip–said more than any words spoken. His gaze was drawn to the glistening wetness of her lips before finally seeking out her eyes.

"It feels right to me, too," he whispered.

Needing to avoid his probing and unable to build effective defenses, she looked away, starting a nursery rhyme in her mind.

"You've been out of it for quite a while." On impulse, he traced her face with the tip of a finger. *Skin so soft to the touch.* "I've been trying to wake you for some time."

She jerked away as if his touch burned.

To resist further temptation, he put more distance between them. "For security reasons, I thought it best not to bring any of your belongings here. Everything you need is either in the closet or the dresser."

Crossing to the side of the room, opening a single door, he pointed out the walk-in closet. Then he gestured to the Queen-Anne, tall dresser on the opposite wall. "The bathroom is through this door right here." He touched the frame of the door beside the closet. "Why don't you freshen up? And I'll take you downstairs."

Allison scooted up into a sitting position, hugging her legs tight to the torso. Meeting him at that house with Debbie and Jake continued to be the last thing she remembered. A chin fell to rest on her knees as a nasty feeling rose.

The reason for Will bringing her here couldn't be good.

Chapter Five

Across several state lines stood a quaint coffee shop on the outskirts of Washington, DC. Other tightly clustered shops were positioned on either side and trailed along three city-block lengths before abruptly ending in a rural setting.

Special Agent Rebecca Patterson (GS-5) sat on a rustic metal and wood stool in front of a high, farm-house-style countertop facing the storefront. Looking out the window, she blew across the top surface of a bright blue ceramic mug and sipped on hot tea while contemplating her recent setback.

Being the youngest of five children made one strong. Especially in her case, since all the rest were born male, one generation removed from the Irish shores, and in an Irish Protestant household.

It was not an easy task for the baby girl of that clan.

Five years ago, it had become even more difficult.

While turning twenty-two, fresh out of Harvard with a legal degree with honors, she enrolled in the FBI academy.

And quite expectantly, all hell broke loose.

Her brothers pulled a campaign inundated with relentless badgering. Even going so far as to pull rank within the academy's personnel, creating all kinds of roadblocks and difficulties that successfully outmaneuvered many of their foes. But not her.

It was only until they got down and dirty sneaky, with a distraction involving their parents, that her focus almost derailed.

Although luck would have it, they didn't win.

So, with a quiet determination that remained unshakable ever since she made her dream happen.

Now, throwing the pleated, auburn braid to the other shoulder, she sat fuming after work in the ordinarily bustling – but now almost empty–cafe around the corner from her new apartment. Her murmuring complaints got expelled on the steaming surface of her cup. "Working twice as hard as any other cadet in the class only gets you so much." She blew on the liquid, helping to cool down her beverage and temperament.

"So what if I'd rode a desk for three long years! Doing the time."

Her cup made a loud clink when set on the tabletop, and the emptiness of her surroundings allowed her to continue venting. "Taking any and every low-ranking duty that came my way. With a freaking smile!" she hissed while her gaze zeroed in on the front door. "Not much matters when the Patterson's' super soldiers decide to interfere."

The source of some of that frustration came striding in with a single-purpose focus–a family trait–and plopped down on the stool across from her. "Hey, Sis." Sean Patterson grinned while tugging on her braid.

"Don't Sis me. It's really low to pull a stunt like this, Sean. I worked hard for that promotion, and thanks to all of you, I'm stuck back at the desk."

In his experience, a tirade had to be fully expelled from her system before a word could get in edgewise. Letting her vent for a few more minutes, he interrupted when the heated temper steamed down to a small coffee percolator instead of an overheated tea kettle. "You were not passed over. You are being re-assigned to something else."

Quickly spotting when that got her attention, he pulled an envelope from the back pocket and slid it across the table in front of her Chai Tea. "This is your contact. The security level is Top Secret SCI. James, Brian, Josh, and I got your back."

"Sensitive Compartmented Information? What's going on?" Rebecca palmed the thick package. Knowing to review it later, she tucked it into the gun harness under her blazer.

The Patterson brothers were an outsourced consultant team with top clearance for a few selected clients. If they got brought on board, something big stood in the works. The fact they included her in it made Rebecca feel proud–but not for long.

Again, her Irish pale creamy complexion flooded with an angry-red blush. The jaw tightened, and forest-green eyes sharpened to a fiery glare.

She looked like a very pissed-off pixie from Ireland's magical shores.

Already in telepathic sync–because of their strong family ties–Sean shook his head no. "We didn't do this. The higher-ups decided, and we gave them the thumbs up."

"Gee, thanks, big brother. Why don't you make all my big decisions for me?"

"If we did, you wouldn't have gotten involved with that stick-up-the-butt college professor and wasted five months of your life."

"Hmm, point taken," she said while gazing at the ceramic mug. If the brothers ever found out how distracted she had become and not with the college professor, they all thought. *Things would go nuclear.* "What now?" Her finger traced around the rim of the cooling drink.

"You follow out your orders and wait for contact."

Sean hesitated briefly before tapping twice on the table near her cup. "And Sis... just a warning, some of what's in there will be hard to read. If you need me-" He pointed to the forehead, signaling for their internal connection.

"Copy. Are you going to be at Sunday dinner?"

"Are you kidding? Mom and Dad would kill me if I took away prime grandkid quality time. Jess would kill me, too. She looks forward to the R&R."

Rebecca grinned. Jesse, Sean's wife, just had a boy and became fiercely protective of her girl time. Even if consuming wine was off the table for a while, Jesse could still enjoy the camaraderie. And, of course, smoke them all in their ongoing bird-watching competition. After all, she wouldn't be hindered by the alcohol intake like the rest of them until baby Ryan weaned off nursing.

"Well, okay then, tell the rest of the Musketeers they're off the hook." She winked while jumping down from the cafe stool. Leaning over, she kissed his cheek before hurrying out, returning to her somewhat empty apartment filled with three tiers of moving boxes. The envelope tucked close to her chest became the priority, so reading it provided another delay for unpacking again tonight.

****

The silence filled the safe house's bedroom with heavy tension. Allison's vulnerability hit Will in the gut, real hard, like a sucker punch.

His hand rose, tightly fisting to press on his stomach as he struggled with a clear path forward, anticipating how hard this was going to be on both of them.

Their ending had come in a similar fashion to every other aspect of their relationship. And explosive passions like theirs came with casualties. Will took a deep breath to loosen the tight muscles in his chest and stomach. When the exhalation came out in a slow release, his resolve strengthened.

This predicament was his fault, after all. Adding fuel to her stubborn belief that their association came with too many risks. So, if he had to suck it up and muddle through, he would do it.

"When you get moving around, you'll notice you're not as steady as you think." With the stubborn tilt of her chin, he came closer. "Or I'll just sit down next to you, and we can talk here." Will patted the space nearby.

His wanting to be near her had him wishing she would resist. He willed her eyes to meet his and, after a small hesitation the silence increase between them as they continued to stare at one another.

Both struggled with their physical awareness, and each attempted to determine the other's intentions by reading their expression and body language.

Allison didn't possess nearly the strength of the two in either of those areas. So, she broke contact first.

"All right," she capitulated. And she added the precaution of resuming a nursery rhyme loop in her head.

"I promise you. It will be okay," he said while approaching her. The uncertainty flashing again across her face burned him with guilt.

Allison flipped the quilt aside and swung her legs over the edge of the bed. As she got ready to stand, a pause resulted when she found herself in a modest–but skimpy nightgown. The glaring reprimand lost its effect as her balance suffered.

Rising too fast and still feeling the sedative's effects made the room spin. Allison's hand flung out to stop herself from falling. The side table rattled, but a masculine hand settled the wobbling lamp just before any damage happened.

Then, just as swiftly, Allison was swept into a strong set of arms. Still reeling, her head fell back onto Will's shoulder, waiting for the world to cease spinning.

"I figured this might happen," Will clarified as his focus pulled to the pair of lips just inches away. He stopped short of the bathroom, studying every characteristic of the face that still appeared in his dreams most nights. It stood out starkly pale now, and the meekness in allowing his hold didn't go unnoticed. All told signs of her present state.

A deep frown accompanied him; stepping inside, he gradually set her down. His hands gently grasped her elbows, holding on until she could stand independently.

Upon his nearness, she took a slow survey of those striking facial contours, stopping at the nose. She couldn't risk going any further. "I'm fine now. You can let me go." An iciness coated her request.

This made him grin. "Understood, but call me when you're finished. I'll come and get you." He guided her to the edge of the sink and countertop.

She sighed and gave a conceding acceptance with a regal tilt to her chin.

Will chuckled at her persnickety manner–the blaring hints of her clawing back to a fighting form. He stepped out but left the door slightly ajar.

"Great," she muttered. The toggle switch to turn on the exhaust fan and provide a sound buffer seemed miles away. "I'm just supposed to go to the bathroom, knowing you're out there listening to everything!"

"Turn on the water," he added patiently from the other side.

Twisting on the faucet with much force, she silently called him many unflattering names. Big Muscled Buffoon became one of the lesser offensive ones.

"Maybe you should think about Mary and her little lambs again," Will suggested while holding back another chuckle.

"Stop getting into my head!" Even knowing that sticking out one's tongue seemed childish, Allison did it anyway.

When the whooshing sound of water stopped, Will knocked, and a muffled reply told him to enter. As the door swung open, his attention jumped to her leaning against the wall, patting her face with a towel. A quick push off the wall had her standing straight and tucking the towel back on the bar.

While trying to move around him unassisted, she stumbled. And Will abruptly lost patience, swore, and scooped her back into his arms.

Damn, the stubborn female. Does she want to fall and harm herself just to prove a point?

Allison crossed her arms defensively tucking her head full of tumbling locks toward his chest, she kept her body rigidly frozen. But even with her glaring displeasure, it became hard for Will to ignore the soft fragrance and curves held in the cradle of his arms.

Thankfully, all too soon, Allison got plopped down in a blue wingback chair by a fire.

The large room with a Cathedral ceiling contained a chill that seeped into the skin. Goosebumps appeared almost instantly after being released. Allison skimmed her hands along the exposed areas to generate heat.

Will tossed some additional fuel on the dying embers and shifted the logs around to get the flames to catch. Once satisfied, he crossed over to the seating arrangement and got an afghan.

Coming toward her, holding out the blanket, she loudly sighed. "Please stop reading my mind. I can't keep up with the stupid rhymes right now, and you're taking unfair advantage."

He laid the soft material across her, tucking it behind the shoulders. The back of his hand lifted and traced the line of her jaw. "No mind tricks needed. I just assumed you'd be chilled in your cute pajamas." Continuing to trace her features, he brought his face closer.

Allison shivered and lurched back, digging deeper into the chair's upholstery.

But not quick enough to prevent Will from feeling that trembling reaction. A mixture of confusion with traces of something else played across her expression. Will paused before rising to stand. He hovered near and softly spoke, "Can I get you something warm to drink? A cup of tea?"

An unclear memory of Allison's floated to the surface with that prompt. Where Will had carried a tray of Bloody Mary drinks into a brightly lit sunroom. And she had been pressured into drinking one by Jake and Debbie.

Allison's eyebrows rose intensely when no other memory came afterward, and a suspicion dug in deep.

What is Will up to?

Chapter Six

Will chuckled and got amused with Allison's blatant suspicion. "Nothing, but tea will be added this time." His head tilted to the side. "Although I think you take it with honey and cream. Do you want me to see if they're available?"

Still wary, she hesitated.

"I promise, Allison. I won't add anything other than milk and honey." His expression was friendly. Sincere.

With a parched throat, she would need something to soothe it if they were to talk. "Okay. Yes, tea, please."

"I'll be right back." Will jerked his chin down.

Allison slowly nodded in agreement and followed his progress into the kitchen.

Her interest in the surrounding space became second nature. Needing a slight reprieve, she allowed her eyes to roam the room's features and studied the competition.

No way is this done by the homeowner.

It wasn't hard to recognize a fellow professional's handiwork. The millwork masterpiece alone–connecting the kitchen to the room she occupied–was a work of art.

This island had dark cherry cabinets with an off-white-colored granite top. Open shelves spanning floor to ceiling were mirrored at each end, and a wood-paneled beam structure extended above the island to interrupt a cathedral ceiling.

Plus, the impressive built-ins with its massive, arc-shaped countertop grouped upholstered stools evenly spaced on the sitting area side. With their high backs, softly padded attached cushions in soft blue and slanted footrests, Allison could see herself occupying any available seats.

Except for the fact that Will stood on the opposite side while completing a task.

The harsh, whooshed sound of pressurized water ran briefly before abruptly ceasing. With the spigot turned off, the tea kettle was lifted in his grasp.

Will's hair fell into his eyes, and he brushed the interfering strands aside. Usually, those thick, almost-black locks got worn short in the back and sides to tame the bane of having a natural wave. But now they were longer and the front even more so. The wavy disarray kept falling over his eyes with the length parted to the right. And that ruffled appearance as if his hands had run through it many times–begged Allison's fingers to touch their softness again.

He glanced up, met her gaze, and smiled.

When Allison quickly looked away, his grip on the handle tightened. He moved beyond the great room's visibility with swift, cutting strides. A loud BANG as the kettle dropped on the burner gave away Will's frustration as he twisted the range's knob to a high setting before searching through the cabinets.

As unrestrained rummaging sounds happened out of direct view, Allison switched to the surrounding area. Her designer's eye absorbed the rich, soft greens and blues sprinkled throughout a soothingly dominant neutral palette. Various quirky and fun accents were mixed with functional pieces covered in inviting textiles.

These areas sought to invite rather than intimidate, and she especially admired the tastefully done seating arrangements, where the smaller, intimate settings were perfectly balanced among the more significant social assemblies. It took experience to get that right, and achieving this was much harder than it looked.

Eventually, Allison's absorption in the decor allowed Will to silently move across hardwood floors and plush area rugs with a tray. The thump of setting it down on the table made his presence known. His stomach twitched with the acknowledgment that she was truly here and not going anywhere for a while.

Pushing a small table and the other chair flanking the fireplace closer, he sat opposite her.

"Gee, isn't this cozy," she sarcastically said. Her eyes zeroed in on the food like she wanted to snatch it up and inhale it lickety-split.

Will tried to hold back the smirk.

Allison's stomach internally grumbled, but she yanked her gaze away from the nearby tempting offerings.

"Why don't you eat and drink while I explain what's going on?" His request got a predictable response. Allison tightly folded her arms on her chest while pretending to ignore the drink and sandwich. A bite to the inside of his mouth stopped a chuckle when she flopped back in the chair with a loud huff.

"I can't go into many details for security reasons, but you deserve to know a little of what's happening." He took a deep, calming breath and began to explain. "I've been a part of an ongoing investigation that originally started as a sting operation to apprehend a string of burglaries concerning historical artifacts."

Allison closed her eyes and said, "Yeah, I remember Civil War stuff." He had been working on this case when they had parted ways. Her uncle hadn't wanted Will to take the job and thought his niece could change Will's mind. Little good was done, sharing her unease. Will's decision never altered.

Not wanting to dwell on that bit of history, Allison added, "You're also a big collector." Her eyelids flickered open.

"My family started the collection. I added to it over the years. Anyway, the investigation started with break-ins to some private collections. However, the thieves broke into prominent national parks with museums soon after the smaller private collectors' burglaries."

Will shifted in the chair, raised a foot, and rested it against the opposite knee. The foot began to swing back and forth to a rapid rhythm. "The National Parks Services asked if I wanted to consult on the investigation. My family has one of the country's largest private collections of Civil War artifacts."

"Ah, Yes. I recall you telling me that once," Allison said while shifting toward the fire's glowing embers. "He was a Confederate spy. He was involved in a big battle during the war... right?"

"Yes, a Secret Service agent at City Point, Virginia. My family kept many of the documents and items from that time and added to them. I became a big collector of the swords and military arsenals, so I'm familiar with the artifacts of that time."

Her very expressive eyes closed with a bombardment of memories. Will did not do anything by half measures. If an interest sparked, he would discover everything there was to know while pursuing it.

At one time, she had caught his avid interest.

Allison promptly came back to the present when Will loudly cleared his throat.

"Having been written up at least a half dozen times in newspaper articles now and again, the Park Services knew of my interest. Since I was consulting for them already with my security company, they approached me to be a part of the team concerning the thefts. That was three years ago. "

"Will, you forget we were together then. I know-"

"This needs to be said. I didn't tell you everything." His voice rose in volume.

"Hmm, what a surprise," Allison heavily puffed out.

He opened his mouth, then closed it. Combing fingers through his hair helped with maintaining some patience. Barely.

Did he believe this wouldn't come up? After all, she had a valid point.

Will sighed before moving on in a calmer voice. "When it fell into the Park Service jurisdiction, I got a lead on the small group behind the thefts through my collector's sources. I devised a plan, but it took some time to set up, and we were just about to set the trap when it morphed into something else entirely.

"Do you remember the attempted break-in with the National Archives Museum? It happened that spring, during the grand opening of the Civil War exhibit."

Nodding, indicating yes, she then looked away toward the fire again. Because of her uncle, Senator Phillip J. Buchanan's connections, she had gotten an invitation but declined. Their relationship had ended two months before, and Will would most likely be in attendance. It would hurt too much to see him in person again.

There were other reasons, as well.

Primarily my delicate condition.

But Allison did scout through all the papers for glimpses of photos and news about him. She remembered the articles about the break-in, but all the focus had been on Will. Unfortunately, he hadn't been alone in the images. He was with the woman who successfully got Allison out of the picture in more ways than just that night's event.

Allison shot a quick look toward Will before looking away. A nursery rhyme started back up in her mind–not wanting to discuss that particular topic anytime soon.

Will frowned when a verse from Mother Goose got pushed into his thoughts. Shaking his head to dispel the nonsensical distraction, he added tighter shields to keep her out.

"Well, when they tried-" Will's foot bounced at an increased tempo when he continued, "the break-in was a bust. They couldn't get into the secured area they wanted. I had added an undeveloped secondary program. Not on the market yet. In case they went for the exhibit. We had hoped it would trigger a tracking program and lead us back to the culprits.

"Unfortunately, that didn't happen. But their attempt shed light on the caliber of talent we were dealing with. Plus, it brought up something nagging me about the thefts. Why would a small group go after that big of an exhibit?"

Shifting again, Will lowered his foot off a knee to the floor. He moved the palms of his hands to the front of the upper thighs, pressing into the jeans' fabric. His repeatedly skimming motion across the surface eased some tension.

"Their previously stolen items could have easily been fenced and sold to a novice collector or on the upper levels of the black market. That wouldn't have been the case with the items held in the Archives. Those would be too hot and too well known to sell in the same way." Resting elbows on the upper thighs, Will leaned forward with his hands folded together, out in front.

"It made sense then why the other stolen items had been untraceable. They weren't selling them. Because of this, I had assumed they wanted the artifacts for their historical worth—not financial."

"That is one serious collector," Allison commented, shifting deeper into the chair.

"Exactly," Will agreed. "Also, it's important to mention that while this investigation was progressing, the FBI approached me about transferring to Washington, DC.

"My company holds contracts with some security software for them. With the attempted burglary of the National Archives, the FBI became the lead investigator. I was asked to relocate and work with another computer consultant. As well as liaison between the two divisions."

"Okay, Will, it's obviously a complicated investigation." Allison wearily rubbed her forehead. "But what am I doing here? I don't collect, nor do I have any desire to start. And… why would my clothes be a security risk?"

"Yes, well, I'm getting to that." He took a slow sip of tea and chose his following words carefully.

"Known for attending functions surrounding my collection interests, I started participating in a few more and brought a date. One Park's Services team member infiltrated the burglary ring using some of my connections.

"Socializing with the collectors allowed her to brush elbows with the parties involved. We made it look like she was using me for my connections and would be willing to play both sides if the price was right. It worked, too."

Allison's body stiffened as the implication began to seep in. "She?" Her voice spoke softly and could barely be heard over the crackling of the nearby fire.

Chapter Seven

Will combed fingers through his hair. At the same time, Allison's posture remained tense.

"Yeah, well. Ah, this part is where you... ahh, misunderstood things.

"When the FBI became involved, they added their own mole, and we thought it best not to tell the one that originated on my team. And we discovered that the original player had been working with the thieves, and more importantly, the group financing their operation."

He tilted his head from side to side and slumped back heavily into the chair with a loud snort of disgust. "Real facts got leaked. And the heists became only a fraction of what was really going on."

"Drugs?" Allison leaned forward, a cup of tea paused in hand before her mouth.

Shaking his head in reply, he continued, "Anyway... the FBI's plant got tight with the players. So close that the partial operation became disclosed. The stakes went up when the new operative told us the latest information. What started as a five, maybe eight-member team and one division morphed into a twenty-five-member group.

"And now, the teams span across several government divisions, with the sting operation becoming something entirely different. The National Park Service is continuing with the original artifact's larcenies.

"Many other teams within the FBI, Homeland Security, and the CIA were assigned to handle the new problem that affects our nation's security."

"What new problem?" Allison asked again. Too engrossed in the story, she forgot about her food strike and started eating a sandwich.

However, Will did notice and couldn't stop his smile from showing as she practically inhaled the food. "Can't tell you." The golden flecks in his eyes danced, understanding her dilemma. He got up and squatted before the fire to fuss with the burning logs.

The embers crackled and flickered, showing abstract shapes in the flames. The room remained still, with only the fire's snapping and popping, filling the silence before Will started talking again.

"Because of my connection to the field operative that defected, the FBI disclosed the findings of their investigation. They were taking steps to remove the operative from the team and wanted it to look like we knew only of their larceny involvement."

Will swiveled around to meet Allison's gaze. "It worked well in one aspect, and a trap became successful due to our past relationship."

Switching back to the fire. He stoked the embers for several seconds before continuing. "I was no longer involved in the Park Service investigations and transferred to an undisclosed area engrossed in consulting and research basis... and forgot about her."

For a brief moment, Will's thoughts cycled inward.

"Her?" Allison prompted.

He shifted his attention to the floor by her chair. The tone of his voice grew low. "I did not know and had only been recently notified after the interrogations that she had been fixated on me.

"My betrayal set her off. Believing one person stood in the way, she wanted to eliminate her competition." His gaze rose and clashed with ones that held confusion.

Allison's head tilted to one side, and she started to comment.

Holding up a hand to stall, he pressed on, "Allison, the original player I'm talking about is Nancy Johnson."

A gasp escaped her lips. "My God. But... she was-"

"Let me finish," Will interrupted. "I introduced her to you at my company's Halloween gala several years ago. The sting operation had been in its beginning stages."

"But that would mean-" Allison spurted out.

Not letting her finish, he rushed to explain, "When the team thought it would play out to our advantage if Nancy and I appeared to be dating to suit the sting, we did. It was all for show. We were just co-workers, nothing more," Will continued explaining.

"You, ah," she sputtered. "Made me believe-" Allison hissed, her fingers pressed against trembling lips. She halted that telling weakness.

"No. I never made you believe anything." Will's features grew rigid. "I didn't cheat. But we needed to make it look like that. I tried to get you to understand, but you wouldn't talk to me. Then, after several attempts with no results, I just stopped trying. You suggested we cool things down, and I transferred to DC."

If Allison could read minds, she would have seen Will's heavy regret and guilt with what went down between them.

A burst of air came out of Will's mouth as he shrugged his shoulders. "Then, Nancy suggested, and everyone agreed that our break-up would make Nancy and my fictional relationship seem even more real. So I went along with the farce."

"Oh, I'm sure she did. That. Conniving-" Allison struggled out of the afghan to stand. Shaky movements made getting free of the blanket hard. The table got bumped, and everything began to tip over.

Intercepting the sliding tray, he pushed the table aside to stand. As Allison's body vibrated with suppressed fury, his feet got anchored on either side of her legs. He kept her in place by squatting, getting to eye level, and resting both forearms on her knees.

"You deliberately allowed me to misunderstand! You keep conveniently forgetting that I can't read your mind as you can mine! I'm done with this," Allison announced.

"You're staying put." He pressed both hands on her upper thighs.

A pair of witch-hazel eyes glared a fiery promise of payback. Stiff body language put Allison's showcasing ire on full display. But she did stop her squirming. The jerked movement against the chair's high back caused the chair to skip backward.

"Allison, Nancy is presently in confinement. However, she has powerful connections, and has some pull with hazardous men. Because of her, there is a contract out on your life."

Her arms quickly uncrossed. Pressing her hands to her chest, Allison shouted, "Me? Why the hell would she do something like that?"

"Because-" Will gritted his teeth. "Damn it. You're being purposely obtuse." He sighed heavily.

If it was at all possible to become even more rigid, she succeeded. While straightening up in her chair, Allison did a passable impersonation of a seventeenth-century queen ready to summon the command to chop Will's head off for daring to displease her.

"Don't go regal on me, your highness." Will harshly ran fingers through his hair again, pulling it back from his face. "Nancy is convinced we both still have strong feelings for each other. Two of my men have been watching and guarding you, and they stopped two attempts on your life in the past two weeks.

"The FBI decided to put you into protective custody." Will left out just how big of a fuss he had made to get involved in her protection.

"But this." Allison waved her arms around, encompassing the room. "Is not necessary."

"How do you figure that?" Will asked with a sharp clipping bite to it.

"Well, one of the supposed attempts was just the slashing of two car tires. Like I told Jake and Debbie, it wasn't even my car. I was traveling on business and using a rental. The other became an unfortunate mugging in the city," she explained. "I think you may be reading too much into those incidents, perhaps overly cautious."

God. Her stubbornness to keep a supposedly normal life holds no bounds. Did she really believe her Uncle... or would I leave her without protection all this time? That we wouldn't know what she got up to... Every. Single. Day?

Taking a deep breath, he quickly let it out. "Someone set a small explosive to go off when you turned on the ignition. One of my men slashed your tires to prevent you from driving the car. He pointed it out to you before you could get into it."

Will leaned closer to her before expanding, "And a few days later, what you believed to be a simple mugging was a successful intervention by a bodyguard after he spotted a man with a gun. His quick thinking probably prevented you from getting a bullet to the head! Not to mention the intruders we intercepted back in Chadds Ford!" Will blurted out in frustration.

Her face lost all its color, and her eyelids closed tightly shut. Flashing memories of her parents came to mind.

The safety and well-being of those around him meant everything to Will. He'd put himself in harm's way to project a stranger in a heartbeat; just don't ask him to sugarcoat things when carrying out that objective.

Will blew out a breath and touched the pressure point of his temple with open palms. He was tired physically, and the lack of sleep made it worse. *But that is no excuse.* "I'm sorry, Allison." Will leaned up and stroked her hair. "I shouldn't have told you like that."

"No." Allison opened her eyes, but her mind was elsewhere even as she looked straight ahead. "I want the truth. But I just can't believe-" A sigh interrupted. When their gazes met, she wondered if one could escape a family curse.

His throat suddenly tightened, and he looked away. After clearing his throat, and twisting back, he said, "This evolved into something we didn't count on. But you are perfectly safe here."

"What about you?" she asked softly. "Will you be careful when you go back?"

"I'm staying here for a while."

Her eyes darted away past him. "There is no reason for you to stay."

"Why don't you finish your tea and sandwich?" With a negative shake of Allison's head, he gathered up the meal and moved the table further away from the chair.

"A few items need my attention, and then I'll be back." Will smiled and added, "I can't disclose everything, but I'll try to answer any question you might have. Okay?"

"Sure. Okay." She blew out a long exhale. The lie had fallen easily from her lips, knowing things were far from okay.

Chapter Eight

Will didn't talk about Guardians Inc.'s business with Allison.

Ever.

So she had very few details regarding his company. Only with what information obtained from their initial meeting at one of her uncle's functions came to mind.

The admiration for the company's success exploding into fruition during Will's final year of college had coated every word of her uncle's voice. Even the start-up cost that came from a small bequeath left by Will's paternal grandmother was a topic of interest within the circle of her uncle's associates.

When having met Debbie and Jake at that same party, Will's office in Conshohocken, Pennsylvania, came up in conversation regarding the newly finished renovation project.

And more recently–thanks to reading a Forbes magazine at a doctor's visit for Sara–Allison had picked up a few more snippets of information. The former State Senator to Maryland, James T. Maxwell, was what drew her eye, posing with his son on the front cover. The tagline, 'Powerhouse,' had indeed summarized the story and became one of the many avenues that announced Will's father as the Guardians, Inc.'s new COO.

At the time of the article, Will's small start-up had grown. The business consisted of 80,000 clients across the U.S and worldwide, with corporate sites located in DC, New York, Denver, Seattle, LA, and a small satellite office in Paris, France.

The article also mentioned that Guardians Inc. specializes in security stuff: computers, personal protection, and security systems. But she had no clue what those things meant past the surface descriptions.

When explaining a workday, Allison had riled him numerous times with the cloak-and-dagger precautions. There got to be even less of an explanation when he went away for a high-ranking client. Government-related.

Had he been shielding me from the dangers of his job? Her chin dropped to rest on her chest.

She had made light of it then, but the evasion had hurt deep down. "I certainly didn't help matters much when I kept pushing him to talk about it." A soft sigh escaped as her shoulders drooped. There also remained a deep regret on how she handled learning of his unique abilities when he finally revealed them to her. Her methods had resulted in his further avoidance, creating an even larger communication gap.

It had made it very easy for Nancy to wedge them further apart.

Not to mention her growing concern about getting in too deep regarding their relationship and the Buchanan curse striking again. It didn't matter that Will's gift looked invincible. With the added level of danger surrounding this world of powerful giants, there was a greater chance of someone getting hurt. Or worse.

Unfortunately, a persistent factor between them hadn't changed this time either, making it very hard to think. She couldn't let this ever-present physical attraction cloud her judgment. Allison's heart savagely thumped. Her hand moved up to press on the erratic pounding when acceptance clinched.

To lose sight of what could happen when your defenses got lowered, courted pain. The past had burned her too many times to ignore those life lessons. Everyone eventually left, either by their actions or by a tragic twist of fate.

Keeping her emotional distance kept a figurative 'bullseye' off the ones she loved.

With that sobering fear and the drug's effects still coursing through her system, a lack of energy caused Allison's eyelids to drift shut. After a brief moment, they gradually opened. Only to have the next blink last for a longer interval as the lids flickered and struggled to rise. Her hand dropped to lay unmoving on a blanket-covered lap. The eyelids, feeling so heavy, finally conceding, remained closed while her breathing became deep and relaxed.

Approaching footsteps carried through the quiet space. Only the occasional pop and hiss of the fire interrupted the sound of fast-moving strides. Until the hard, thumping rhythm came halfway into the room and suddenly stopped.

Allison had settled back to sleep. The afghan hung loosely around the waist and legs. With feet tucked under her to one side, her hands folded loosely on the nearest thigh.

Will felt himself getting sucked back into that unsettling vortex. Never in his life did he struggle so much to curb these possessive tendencies. These intense feelings kept pushing his boundaries, eating away his caution.

Before meeting Allison, he thought loving a woman was a pleasant endeavor. That natural step one took to reach adulthood. But his experience with his ex-fiancé, Rachael, seemed a pale imitation of what he felt for Allison.

His eyes swept across every detail of her face.

She looked so young.

That admission would only annoy her.

Often mistaking her twenty-eight years as much younger, people underestimated her. And just like him, they ended up with their unfortunate outcomes in doing so. But he wouldn't make that mistake again.

He leaned down and carefully gathered her up into his hold. She stirred briefly before contently settling into his protective embrace.

There would be no more talking for them tonight.

****

A few hours later, Will sat alone in the main study, adjacent to the great room that Allison had occupied earlier, finishing up a call.

He had been trying to finish up on some business leads before addressing the latest snag in this investigation.

"Yeah, Sean. The new software was a bust. It didn't trace the call as we had anticipated. Maybe they were using an unknown blocking program." Will sat back, listening to Sean Patterson speak the nerd language only a fellow coder would understand. His head bobbed up and down, agreeing with what his collaborating private consultant contributed.

His fingers kept flicking the antique gold coin his grandfather gave him on the desktop. The image of a floating eye centered within a pyramid blurred with the coin's spinning movement. Will carried this coin everywhere and even incorporated the strange design as his company's logo.

He pressed down on the quarter-sized disk, and the one face with the all-seeing eye clinked on the wood surface. Not liking his thoughts, the world's weight seemed to press inward.

"You'll have to dive deeper into the coding perimeters to see if it can be fixed. I have too many fires to put out as it is." Will sighed before adding, "Give me a call when you figure something out."

The call ended with the omission of any social pleasantries. It was an everyday occurrence when they got into the nitty-gritty of the technical process. Not many others could hold their own with these two experts when it came to the latest programs and inventions within the security field.

As a thriving business owner, he was used to long work hours, seldom stopping. Hell, the word, downtime wasn't a concept he understood. Working as a lead consultant on this investigation, remaining an active CEO of his company, and juggling other investment holdings didn't run itself. And sleep resulted only when it couldn't be avoided.

But what happened a few moments ago–initiating his call to Sean kicked it up a notch.

Rubbing his face briskly, Will held back a headache. He didn't know what else to do about the problematic phone conversation playing on a continuous loop in his head.

And, in one way, it gave a much-needed diversion. This burning need to keep Allison safe curtailed other distracting thoughts. His mind stopped drifting–at least, not too many times–to their earlier kiss.

Two quick hits to the thick paneled door followed by its abrupt opening had Will look up to lock gazes with Resident Agent in Charge (GS-14)-with the FBI. "What's rolled in?"

Jeffrey Collins, Will's best friend, partner, and bodyguard–all rolled in one–closed the door and flipped the lock. "It sounds serious." Agent Collins came striding forward. Nudging Will further away from the desk, he leaned on the top surface.

Will sighed while pushing Jeff's butt off long enough to collect the files he had been reviewing. Being very familiar with his friend's approach to desks, tables, and counters in place of chairs, Will lost that argument long ago.

Jeff took no offense, settled back down, and tucked his hands into the front pockets of his jeans.

His nickname, "Surfer," perfectly suited him because of his pro-surfing back in the day and a continuing habit of speaking in surfer slang. Not to mention a tall, lanky frame, shaggy blonde hair, and sea-blue colored eyes certainly fitted that beach-boy stereotype.

This layback persona coated everything he did. Until it didn't.

And when that switch flipped you got out of his way.

Leaning back into a chair, his arms reaching upward in a stretch, Will took a deep breath. As he exhaled, he popped back forward and dropped the bad news. "Nancy called me. She's escaped."

"What the-?" Jeff stood straight up.

"I confirmed it," Will interjected. "While letting her stroll around the facility after dinner, two guards were shot, and she got away clean."

"Who would authorize that for a restricted prisoner?" Jeff rubbed the palm of his hands roughly along the face. The two-days without shaving only added fuel to his roguish appearance. Hands dropped to rest on either side of the hip as he shifted. Their gazes locked. "You know what this means?"

"Yeah, we had another mole."

"Had?" Jeff commented.

"Yeah, ah, had. Nancy let it slip in the conversation."

Catching that slight hesitation, Jeff studied Will's face. "Who was he?"

"I sent an email to the home office while talking to her. I asked them to pick up Agent Thompson for questioning. But who knows what that will get us."

"Akaw! Why would she let that slip? Better to keep him in place for further Intel."

"Maybe he was only there to ensure the breakout, or maybe Nancy was acting alone. Either way, we're dealing with too many maybes. Hell… being such a wild card. Why does Nancy do half the things she does? I can't figure her out."

"Because you're too close," Jeff added.

"How can you say- God damn it! You know how I feel about-"

"Whoa, Brah, ease up on the board. I meant too close to the situation because of Allison. You're not looking beyond it. Sometimes, the wave gets in the face, and all you see is a wall of water."

"Jeff, knock it off! I'm not in the mood for your beach Zen right now."

"Oh, sure. No problem, dude." Jeff winked while barely rubbing the tip of his nose with his middle finger.

Will laughed, loosening some upper body tension. Tilting his head, rotating it back and forth, he relieved the tightness around the neck area. "Nancy said the hit was still on."

Jeff looked up from scanning the preliminary report. With the advantage of rooming with Will in college and the subsequent close bond, Jeff knew all Will's physical tells. "I'll take the lead on Agent Thompson."

A set of eyebrows rose when Will's gaze darted away. Most likely, Will was fighting another bad headache; operating on thirty hours without sleep would do that. Not to mention pushing special abilities past the limits. But Jeff's sixth sense told him otherwise.

So, the white elephant in the room–the apparent omission of pertinent facts–got ignored while Jeff glanced over the unofficial report.

Afterward, when Will's report came to an inconclusive closing, Jeff talked him into taking some migraine medication.

Talk. Threaten–same difference.

The end result would have Will rested and starting back at it in a few hours, which gave Jeff some time to review a couple of things. He headed to his realm, the back security room behind the kitchen.

A clipped pace replaced his usual meandering stroll. His actions held purpose as he sought to get to the bottom of that gut feeling that settled hard in his core. He had no intentions of letting his best friend get caught in a 'Closeout.'

Whatever Will didn't want to say could be the very thing that got him in too deep to come away unscathed.

Chapter Nine

Guardian's Inc.'s intelligence wizardry automatically recorded all incoming and outgoing conversations. Although difficult to access, it did not reach beyond Jeff's expertise. He rapidly typed in codes and reprogrammed the security terminal to find the specific phone call's recording.

Though Will started the tracking program while taking the call, it failed to establish a trace.

Jeff sighed deeply before telling the guard to watch for Will and conduct the upcoming security check without them. He emailed several people to get the information loop constructed regarding Agent Thompson and got to work. He placed the headphones on and played back the recording to get the complete picture.

The phone conversation and security video went as follows:

"Maxwell..."

"Hi, Honey, miss me?"

"Nancy?" Will placed a phone on the desk and pushed the speaker button.

"Don't bother tracing the call, Will. I'll be off in under the required time. I just wanted to tell you not to worry about me, and I miss you. So much, in fact, I want to give you a small token of my affection. You can thank Agent Thompson for his help in my release."

"Where are you? Maybe I can come meet you?" Will typed quickly on a laptop; the mouse dragged on top of the desk surface, and he promptly clicked on the device.

Jeff watched as Will's eyes flared brightly on the monitor—firing up his powerful talent, attempting to establish a connection. Will was the best human phone tap they had available anywhere.

"Oh Will, I'd like that, really I would. But I'm not ready. I need to get everything set up first for your visit."

"Really, like what?"

"A secure location to start. Then arrange for security precautions, of course. You know security is the most important. I mean, you live and breathe it—right, Will?"

Jeff leaned in closer toward the monitor. On-screen, Will broke off the connection to the phone call's data source and rubbed his face. From Will's frown, it became evident that his cyber telepathic link had been unsuccessful, too. As the video played on, Will resumed typing on his laptop before speaking again.

"Yes. I do." A slight pause preceded with Will's following response. "Are you using any of my systems... hardware?"

"Real funny, like I'd tell you that silly. Oh, I forgot."

"Forgot?"

"Yeah, the other thing I'm doing so you can visit with me."

"Okay, what else?" Will asked while quickly typing.

"To make sure, Allison is dead. It's the most important thing."

"That's never going to happen, Nancy." Will's hands fisted above his keyboard briefly, and then resumed typing.

"Never say never."

"What makes you so sure I'll want to visit with you if you manage to succeed? I will not cooperate with you if you harm an innocent bystander."

"Well, I guess we'll have to find an incentive. Like we did with Andrew McKnight."

"The novelist?"

"Yeah. He writes about political theories and stuff like that."

"What do you want with him?"

"Me? Personally, nothing—but to the Copperheads and our employers—he has a purpose. I can't go into it right now, Darling. But soon. I was just telling you about him because we found his incentive. He came in all easy-like. Don't worry, they both like being guests here. You will, too. Gotta go."

"Wait, Nancy, give me something more. I'd like to see it from your point of view and understand. Maybe if I do, we can meet sooner."

"Ahh... You're just trying to keep me on the line. It's not fair using my feelings for you against me. They're waving, I gotta go. Kiss Allison goodbye for me."

The line went dead, and Will leaned forward. He massaged his eyes with his elbows resting on the desk's surface, pressing a face into the open palms.

"What a cluster fuck," Jeff swore.

Pete, one of Guardians Inc.'s agents, swiveled around after the outburst.

"Nothing, Pete-" Jeff gestured to the security monitors facing the back wall.

Tearing off the earphones, letting them fall to the floor, he typed furiously on the keyboard. Only pausing when a few phone calls needed to be made.

After twenty minutes had passed, he stopped and spun back to the monitors, viewing all the rooms. One security camera picked up Will asleep on the leather sofa in the office. Jeff slumped on the desk with a stance miming Will's just after his call with Nancy.

And after all the shit that just got played back, Jeff had a headache too.

****

Suddenly, a pair of forest-green, colored eyes snapped open. Panic set in before her feet could touch the floor. Allison looked around the room and confirmed that last night wasn't a bizarre dream. The dashed pace to the closet door halted when she spotted the number of new clothes available to her in the enormous closet. Her head shook at Will's over-the-top purchases.

A trembling hand hovered near articles of clothing for a second or two before foreboding necessities took precedence. The hand jerked forward, yanking off the nearest items on hangers and snagging a pair of sneakers on an adjacent shelf. Shedding the nightgown and donning the clothes, she pushed her feet into the sneakers without socks.

Back up in a flash, her trek out of the room and her way downstairs went like a blur. The only direction known was where Will had taken her before. When she stopped in the middle of the great room, the familiar surroundings ended.

Two French doors were positioned to the right of the fireplace. She immediately went to the nearest one.

Of course, Will locked it. Her hand shook while fumbling with the latch.

With a resounding click, it swung open. The bubbling panic urged her to move. As she launched outside—as if the Hounds of Hell gave chase, nothing would slow her down.

But no sooner as she caught her stride did a skidding halt take place. Cursing like a sailor, with her potty mouth fully unleashed, she frantically spun in a full circle.

The high, thick shrubs and tall, wrought iron fence surrounded an outdoor terrace with an in-ground pool. Her gaze jumped from one enormous potted plant to the next. The lushness of the colorful florals, pristine landscaping and sparkling clear water all received a skimming glance. But, the gate among the greenery caught her full attention.

That way out got crushed too soon, and she shook the locked barrier in frustration.

Kitchen! Popped into her thoughts.

Hoping there was a back door; she spun away and ran back inside. Just as she reached the house's threshold, a tall, lanky stranger stood in her way, holding a gun aimed upward.

At first, Allison paused in startled shock, and a pitiful squeak escaped.

But what followed afterward became a self-preservation reaction combined with muscle memory from repetitive training. The self-defense lessons–a bargaining chip for getting more freedom from her uncle–taught the skills that came like second nature.

Just ask the man Allison mistook as a mugger last week. It obviously didn't come up in Will's lecture last night, but thanks to her training, that man walked away with more bruises than her.

Too caught up in the present moment, she didn't notice the weapon being lowered.

Her left hand struck out, clasped the pistol around the top of the slide, and pushed it away. At the same time, her body stepped to the side. Once the firearm cleared her person, her right arm wrapped around the gun near the attacker's hand. Then, using this connection, isolating the dangerous item, her momentum moved toward the man, and her right foot kicked upward. Fast and hard. With the hit to the man's groin area, she rocked back on the opposite foot and manipulated the gun from the man's hold to disarm him.

She threw the gun into the pool as the man fell to his knees in excruciating pain, and her roundhouse kick toppled him over.

A swift shimmied dance got her past him to make her way inside. Clearing the path around the kitchen island, she looked back to see if anyone else had come for her.

All remained clear.

She had just swerved back, facing forward, when a dense solid mass instantly stopped any further movement. Strong arms wrapped around her waist prevented a fallback and hard landing on the butt. But that didn't come to mind when she frenziedly fought through a haze of blind panic and adrenaline.

Will's calm, steady stream of reassuring comments did not slow the struggle within his arms.

When her movements faltered, he took advantage. Shifting their bodies, he positioned her against the counter's edge. The safety on his handgun got re-engaged and placed on the nearest surface behind them.

His hold on Allison slipped, and she tried to break free. Her hands got tucked between their bodies while her small frame pressed tight against the cabinet.

She wrestled, twisted, and demanded to be released. Threats spewed from her lips, ranging from bodily harm, getting contracts revoked, and lawsuits.

To no avail, she remained trapped in his arms. And while tiring herself out, Jeff entered the kitchen.

A message got sent using their telepathic link. *I got this.* Will told his friend.

Jeff nodded, shifting slowly, and hobbled back toward the office.

Chapter Ten

Allison remained trembling. Harsh breaths sawed in and out and accompanied the loud sound of rapid heartbeats drumming in her ears. Failing to free her arms from between their bodies, she tried to kick Will's shins. But he had pushed her so tight into the cabinet that movement of any kind became impossible. The strenuous activity of fighting a boulder and not getting it to go anywhere took its toll on her endurance.

She finally surrendered and went still.

"I need you to be calm," Will informed her as the volume of heavy breathing continued to ease. "I've had enough excitement this morning."

"Whatever," she said, muffled. Holding her so tightly, Allison couldn't pull her mouth from his sweatshirt.

"Honey, what got you spooked? Whatever it is, we'll work it out."

"Let up. You're hurting me." She was too pissed to sound helpless.

"Promise me." He waited with as much patience as possible.

"I promise, darn it, I promise. Let. Me. Go!"

Will backed away just enough to give her some space but still close enough to limit her freedom.

"You can't keep me here!" Her air intake started to get elevated again.

His hands moved to settle gently on Allison's shoulders but backed away when she tried to shrug them off. A second afterward, he caught her eyes darting to find an escape route. He quickly eased forward. "Don't even think about it."

Her chin tilted upward. Defiance coated every nuance of her being. And anger took a palpable physical presence, like a molten, heated element simmering and ready to blow. If it were at all possible, flames of fire would have left him a pile of ash on the floor.

The insane urge to press her back and take another kiss washed over him.

"Give me some room," she spoke through grinding teeth. Her words vibrated with a mountain of resentment.

He stepped back, motioning for them to sit in the connecting room.

She adamantly shook her head no. Instead, she moved away and stood in front of the center island.

"Why don't you tell me what you hope to achieve by leaving?" With deliberate movements and a gaze locked to hers, he took a page from Allison's playbook and moved to the countertop's opposite side. The deep island's separation made sense.

She placed both hands, palms facing down, onto the countertop. "If what you said is true, then Nancy's associates know all about my family. They could use them to get to me. Sara-" Her voice broke with heavy emotion. "They can use Sara and my sister to…"

Will remained still, but the desperate need to bridge the gap—rode him hard. His body vibrated with tenuous restraint. If he conceded to those impulses to touch, she would back farther away—both physically and emotionally. Therefore, he tried words.

"Listen to me, Allison. Carefully. I promise your family is safe. The FBI and trusted men from my company are assigned to protect them."

"But they are-"

"We know where they are. Your sister and her family have been made aware of the situation. They're left alone only when in their hotel rooms. Even then, there are guards posted continuously to keep them safe."

"But I need to see them!" The loud clap of open palms hitting against the granite surface filled the room. "Can you understand? Darn it! I can't stay cooped up here with my family exposed to danger."

"You being near them might bring more danger to them," Will explained.

"How can you be so sure?" She looked away.

"You know the answer to that already, Allison."

A piercing look shot back at him as she said, "I want to know why being away from my family is the only answer. You know what? Don't answer that. I want to talk to your supervisor. In fact, I demand to speak to my Uncle. Right now!"

Will sighed and added under his breath, "I'd be better off keeping you drugged."

"I cannot. Believe!" Her body jerked with each word that struggled out. "You- You are-" Her hand slapped the counter. "You cannot possibly... think-" Allison's chin tilted higher, and a haughty allegation swiftly spilled out, "This is not a customary operating procedure for the FBI!"

She pointed a finger toward him and added another accusation, "This is so like you."

Locks of tousled hair partially covered the eyebrows that rose toward his hairline.

"I don't mean that! At least, I hope you don't routinely drug women. I meant making up your mind without discussing it with any associating party, and then you. You. Just do it!"

"Why not contact me at work? Or better yet, have one of the FBI agents contact me?" Allison paused in her ranting to take a deep breath. She began pacing back and forth before adding,

"But no! Instead, you set me up. When I get my hands on Debbie and Jake, I will-" Her hands swung up and outward as she mimicked, throwing a few punches.

Will took this opportunity to get some words in edgewise. "I'm a consultant working with the FBI, not for, so I guess I have a little more maneuvering room than having to follow their standard procedures. I did what was best for all parties, but most importantly, the ongoing operation." Although Will wouldn't share the grey areas, he willingly plowed through to protect her anytime soon.

"Equally important. I thought of your safety. Debbie and Jake didn't know how I would get you to accompany me. They thought they were there to discuss options. But when our meeting place got compromised, I improvised."

Allison stopped her pacing and glared at Will. "I don't exactly remember what happened. But I know you probably tricked me!"

"Whatever," he interrupted. "When you took the drug, we no longer needed to discuss options. It was unfortunate to get them involved like that. But it worked. You are unharmed and here without a lot of uncalled-for attention."

"Uncalled-for attention? What about my clients? Appointments that I've missed?"

"As far as anyone knows, you left for vacation early. You'll extend it for personal reasons when you don't return after two scheduled weeks. Debbie and Jake can take care of your clients while you're gone."

"You will not hold me here for several weeks!" Her palms slammed against the counter again. "It's against the law, Will!"

"Allison, staying as you were... is dangerous. And we can argue all this out now. But I'm not going to apologize for the fact that you're safe while we do it."

"Damn you, Will! You're unreasonable!"

Will gave a negative shake of his head.

They each faced the other in a battle of resolve.

In his stance and most definitely in the eyes, Will would not change his mind. In her first-hand experience dealing with strongly opinionated and overprotective males in most of her upbringing, this current ranting would do no good.

Releasing a slow breath, she recentered the swirling emotions within. The following deep inhale and slow release pushed those negative thoughts aside. If accomplishing her goal failed by calm reason, then other matters would come into play.

But she would cross that bridge only if it was the last resort.

Only one crucial thing mattered: she could not stay here with him. There would be no way she could sustain resistance to her heart's innermost desire.

And too much was at stake.

Chapter Eleven

Once sharp with firm tension, Allison's features became soft in relaxed composure. Skin tone, still flushed, looked less like an apple and more like a peach. With eyes closed and her breaths going in and out, Allison's upper body rose and fell with every inhale and exhale.

"I apologize." Her eyes slowly opened. She blinked a few times before focusing on her ex-lover.

Will's composure slipped, not recognizing this new tactic. He much preferred her hot-headedness. It was easier to outmaneuver her. Clearing his throat, he backed up to lean on the counter.

"Don't look at me that way. I mean it." She laughed, moved to the other side of the island, and sat up on the counter to get closer. Shifting hips and settling down to get more comfortable, Allison let out a long sigh while studying him. "I took my fears and frustrations out on you, not to mention that poor guy back there. I should go apologize."

She swerved toward the patio. "Where is he?"

"He went back to the security room," Will explained.

"Oh. Okay, I'll, um, tell him later." Her petite frame eased around, and her eyes studied Will's expression. "I got upset."

"Understandable." He looped his thumbs inside his front jeans pockets, slowly rocking back on his heels and toes.

Allison's train of thought dissolved.

Will's feet were bare, and she hummed while looking down at them. His deceptively casual posture flagged a blaring alarm in her mind. In the past, that stance signified deep thinking and strategic planning. And back then, she learned to be very nervous about what that meant.

"Allison?" Will interrupted her worrying.

"Hm, right." She dragged her focus off those toes and looked up.

"You've been living with this operation for a while now. Perhaps you thought it best bringing me here."

Will remained quiet. However, his eyebrows raised significantly on that last comment.

She shrugged back. "Bringing me here within a controlled environment-"

"Jesus, Ally!" he interrupted. "You're welcome to go anywhere within this house and its surrounding grounds. I wouldn't control you. Just keep you safe."

A hand came up, motioning for him to wait. "I meant a controlled location versus being elsewhere. You would have had to explain this while protecting me from many unknown variables.

"Adding complications," she conceded.

He nodded in agreement.

"I promise to consider what you have said. However, in exchange, I would like some additional consideration-"

"Allison, I'm not going to-"

"Let me finish first!"

Will roughly rubbed his face. A weary man became exposed when hands dragged through a head of hair to settle on his hips. He wasn't sure whether the lack of sleep got to him or Allison's presence.

She rushed on when he gestured for her to continue, "I would like to call my family and talk to them. Also, reading all the pertinent information you can allow will get me up to speed regarding my situation."

Allison saw his scowl and instantly huffed out, "If I have all the information, I might be able to help"

"No," he softly said.

"But," she added.

Will's hands raised in surrender, not wanting another argument. "I'll give you reports to read. But I don't want you to help or get involved."

"Aren't I already involved?"

Will conceded with a shrug.

"I don't mean help with apprehending them or whatever. But I can help in the research or other harmless activities. I will need something to fill my time here."

"You could just relax and take a vacation," Will suggested.

Allison gave him a you know me, but still suggested that look.

"Once I take the time to read all the information you have to give me, I might return to my original feeling of going home," she forewarned.

"That will not be an option." Will's stance brook no argument.

Biding her time, she shrugged, mimicking his earlier reply.

"Concerning your conditions, which one do you want to do first?" he asked.

"I would like to speak with my family."

"Okay, Ally." He grinned when catching her pursed lips. "We can agree with that direction." When Allison nodded, he added, "However, I will need to outline some ground rules of what you can discuss over the phone."

Her mouth opened to speak, and his hand rose with the palm facing outward.

Holding her off, he said, "It's not open for debate." Will's expression stayed unyielding as his hand was held out, urging her toward the library.

She proceeded in a hurry, eager to resume control of the situation. When the same hand rested on the small of her back, it took everything within her not to pull away.

"There is a slight chance someone could eavesdrop on the calls even though your family received secured phone lines. I'll need to monitor the conversations carefully," he told her as they passed through the library's threshold.

To be paranoid because of the visitors that showed up at the house in Chadds Ford made sense.

They had a leak somewhere, and Will wouldn't trust anyone except a handful of people until they figured out who sold them out.

After guiding her toward the large desk that dominated the room, he pointed out a file with the family's hotel phone numbers and other needed numbers that lay ready and waiting.

Will at least gave her some distance. Pulling out an oversized leather wing chair, he sat down at a small reading table near the back of the room. The thick stack of files scattered across the table surface seemingly took his interest off her.

And with the connection to her family quickly amended and the joint assurances of their well-being–in a disjointed and meandered progress–she paid him no mind, too, except when her lips pressed together at one point in the conversation, and her eyebrows furrowed.

A gaze darted to Will and then down at her hands.

His jaw tightened as he tried not to over-monitor. Not the conversation on the phone but the one in her mind. It took more energy, providing shields to block out people's thoughts than allowing them in.

And when he was tired, it got more complicated.

Like in their past, his mind needed to stay connected to Allison's for some reason. To share the same mind-space with her felt so natural. And because that obsessive need grew stronger the more they were together, he fought against it even harder.

Isn't that why you let her pull away and run to DC? His reprimanding thoughts seeped in. Snapping off that tethering string, he refocused on the files. But when catching the laughter in her voice, he froze mid-task and looked up from the files yet again to watch her.

Allison's hands animatedly moved while speaking. Her shoulders leaned forward, actively listening to the other person's contribution to the conversation. Her head repeatedly tilted to the side in silent response.

A strong sense of déjà vu hit him. That soothing, unguarded release of musical pitches in her uniquely husky voice could always kick-start his desire.

Clueless of his predicament, she smiled, leaning back in the chair, cradling the headset between a shoulder and cheek. The relaxed posture in the chair had wreaked havoc on her coiled bun. Locks of hair brushed across her face, and she impatiently pulled the pencil from its precarious placement. The liquid-like masses of glistening, rich, auburn hues fell upon her shoulders.

Without any power to stop it, his focus again got pulled to her.

She is so beautiful.

His eyes glided over the delicate features that hid a strength of steel below the surface. An undeniable pull kept weaving them tighter and tighter together. Trying to shake it off, a spark of suspicion gained strength on how unescapable the situation had become. He honed in on the nearby discussion like a lifeline.

"No, Peg. She didn't! Oh my gosh, what did the guard do? Did you find the key?" Allison chuckled and eagerly listened to her sister's reply.

Having familiarity with their discussion caused Will to grin. Jeff had laughed about it, too, when reading the report. And the poor agent would never live it down.

Will had to give the child credit for creativeness. If that little girl, Sara, was anything like her mother or aunt, they would have to keep a better lookout. Any sense of security for Allison and her family would evaporate if a three-year-old child could outsmart a team of FBI and Guardians Inc. agents.

While chuckling, Will hooked Allison's awareness.

She immediately stiffened.

"Ahh, listen, Peg, if you want, I can talk to her when she gets back from the pool," she said, dropping her volume to a whisper.

A giggle escaped after getting her sister's reply, and some of Allison's stiffness lessened. Pivoting away and shifting her body in the chair, she kept her tone low, adding, "I'm going to hang up now. Hug everyone for me, and take care. Yes. I will," Allison assured her before adding, "I love you too. Bye."

Swiftly rotating around, a chin pointed upward as her hands tightly clenched. Her eyes shot daggers of pure frustration in his direction. "You are so rude!"

Will shrugged and looked away, back down to the paperwork. He flipped a sheet of paper over and pretended to read the content.

Allison kept her eyes on him when dialing the next call. Her voice remained low, and the dialogue stayed business-related. But through this call, most of her consideration stayed centered on Will. After numerous times of working fingers through his head of hair with his sole interest on the files before him, she relaxed her guard and got preoccupied with work.

Not before long, after losing count of how many phone calls went out, Allison softly laid the receiver on its cradle an hour later.

She needed to relieve tight muscles in the upper shoulder and back area, so she reached her hands high into the air and arched her spine. If one more person, one more time, asked about where she was or when she'd be back, she'd scream. Twisting, she looked in Will's direction while slowly coming out of a stretch.

With hair and ruffled clothes, Will looked like an unruly youth up past bedtime.

Watching him as he slept had always been a favorite pastime. She could study him without worrying about what could be picked up in her head. Moving closer, a frown displaced her thoughtful expression, as little details became noticeable when not battling things out with him.

Will's eyes held dark circles underneath, and his complexion seemed paler.

Carefully lifting the file that rested on his lap, Allison put it with the others. When Will remained soundly asleep, she glanced at her watch and noted 10:15

A sly grin appeared.

Stopping at the door, glancing back–like checking on a sleeping tiger–she turned the knob very slowly and held her breath as the door got urged open as silently as possible.

"I'll just see what I have to work with," she whispered, increasing the distance between them.

Chapter Twelve

Will's body jerked up and out of the chair as he came abruptly awake.

His breathing panted in and out, painfully harsh on his dry throat. Still feeling the effects as he had held Allison as she bled to death, the escaping nightmare still had its claws dug deep in him.

Trying to pull Will back down.

The attack had come out of nowhere in the dream, and he hadn't recognized the area. There had been so much blood swirling around the floating body as he pulled her to shore.

He squeezed his eyes closed, trying to dispel the image of the blood-filled waterway carrying Allison's life force downstream. His heart rate stayed dramatically active. The vital organ wanted to pierce through the muscles and bones of his chest.

It was just a dream, he reassured himself.

Although not like one he had ever had before.

Never had the sense of power been so strong. Shaking his head to dispel the ominous memory, he looked toward the desk, and his heart rate kicked up a notch.

Allison was gone!

Jumping up and heading out of the room, Will shouted for her and anxiously searched the surrounding areas.

After several minutes of shouting, she came out from the kitchen area. Her body looked unharmed as she dried her hands on a kitchen towel. He instantly reigned in his panic.

Unfortunately, the fear changed immediately to anger. "What the hell are you doing? And why the hell didn't you wake me up?"

In reaction, Allison sniffed loudly. She squeezed and twisted the fabric in her hold. "I was under the impression that I wasn't a prisoner here, and I don't like your tone of voice."

Her chin angled higher as she pivoted on her toes and headed back into the kitchen.

Way to go, dumbass, Jeff's telepathic reprimand came through loud and clear.

Will followed her slower, allowing himself time to get his thoughts in gear. Not to mention giving Allison time to cool down. When reaching the kitchen island, Allison stood opposite him, facing the stove. Judging it safe to get closer, he jumped up to sit on the countertop, still leaving her some breathing room.

The dream still had its claws hooked in him. A moment became necessary, so the urge to yell and shake her–passed. The irrational urge to have Allison where he could see her at all times wasn't something he could quickly implement.

At least not without her cooperation.

And that sure as shit isn't happening anytime soon.

So, instead, it was better to sit quietly.

Will briskly rubbed his face in a circular motion. Reigning in dread, he worked out the kinks from sleeping upright in the chair. *Get your brain in gear.* He thought while combing his fingers through his hair.

He tiredly sighed before saying, "You're right." Massaging his temple, he could feel the headache stubbornly holding on, but not as strong.

At first, Allison stood facing the stove with a rigid bearing. After allowing a few moments to pass, she eased around with her stance, relaxing along with her temper.

As Will wrestled with his stress, her attentiveness centered on him.

She approached him with his shoulders slumped and lines of strain sunk deeper around his mouth and eyes. "Why don't you rest a bit more? You look exhausted." Without much thought behind it, her hand on his thigh made soft, soothing, circular motions.

Will slowly opened his eyes and really looked back at her.

Analyzing every inch of what stood before him.

Appearing refreshed, a soft red cashmere cardigan hung loosely open on her shoulders. Her simple, front button-down, pinstripe red and white shirt was paired with a glossy-stretch-twill trouser in dark blue, accentuating her tiny waist.

Only Allison could make this assemblage look exotic, especially with an elaborate knot on top of her head, with decorative hair chopsticks poking out on either side. Some loose strands of titian, silky hair fell around her face.

Damp hair from a recent shower smelled of a fresh spring morning and that unique apple blossom scent. Luring him further down a path he wasn't sure he presently had the right to take.

Her hauntingly lovely features were impossible to forget.

Add in the dedication to work hard at everything. The affectionate nature and funny sense of humor made Allison impossible not to miss when they parted ways.

With a deep breath expelling more tension, he slowly inhaled her tantalizing, soft scent, and another realization hit him.

If anything happened to her or... if he was stupid enough to let her go again, his world would be dismal at best.

Reaching up, he touched the tip of one sparkly, red resin chopstick. The purchase of this item, and many more like it, was made because he remembered how much she had liked them. His smile of simple enjoyment slowly came about, fancying that she wore what he had picked out.

"What time is it?" he asked, needing a distraction from this complication.

"A little past 1:00 pm," she answered. "I was making some lunch for us." She retreated to the range top. A saucepan simmered on low heat. Allison reached out and gingerly turned off the burner. "I... I found some stew in the refrigerator and was re-heating it." While stirring the stew, she angled back to face him.

Will nodded in understanding. "It smells good," he commented, visually outlining every minuscule detail of her expression.

Shifting weight back and forth on each leg, she fiddled with the wooden spoon. "Jeff liked it. He was getting a second helping when you began shouting." She glanced at him and looked away.

Only to be drawn back.

Watching the nervous fidgeting Will shifted closer to her. "Jeff likes everything," he quietly spoke.

They continued studying each other.

Allison couldn't think of anything to say.

"Come here for a minute, Ally."

The fear of something happening to her made Will's head throb more intensely.

He had always called her Ally, either as a form of affection or when wanting to rile. And both had the same outcome. That often led to a bed or... any other suitable surface.

Shivers ran up her spine when some unsuitable places flashed in her memory.

A flush of color rushed to her cheeks.

Allison swung back to the stove. "You know I don't like to be called that." No one except Will ever got away with it. She continued stirring the stew, forgetting it had been turned off already.

"I remember differently." He had silently come up from behind and stilled her hand. Taking the spoon and setting it on the counter, he eased her around. A slow, leaning-down movement brought his lips in touching distance.

A soft, gliding brush moved across her delicate jawline.

Unprepared for this closeness, her voice could not have protested even if she had wanted to.

But her mind did screech out in alarm.

Chapter Thirteen

Will continued to sweep a shiver-inducing path with his lips. "I'm sorry I yelled at you," he whispered against flushed skin. "I panicked when I found you gone." He slowly gathered her close.

Carefully, his hold pressed her face in the nook below his chin so as not to spook her.

"I told you I would gather all the information you promised and then make my decision," Allison stiffly spoke. "Besides, it would be nearly impossible to go anywhere without a mode of transportation. We're not exactly in the center of town."

"I know," he replied, and a hand gently massaged her slim frame. "I guess I overreacted. Blame it on lack of sleep." He felt Allison slowly nodding, still tucked under his chin. Will rubbed slow, soothing circles, coaxing her body to yield to him.

The headache had eased its gripping edge just by holding her. His eyes closed, and he settled into a feeling of contentment, ignoring the reflex to keep his distance.

Allison sighed. The weight of her eyelids seemed to increase and drag them closed. She burrowed further into his shirt and fully relaxed into Will's embrace.

Her slight figure, wearing flats, fit snugly in his arms.

At this moment, she felt so fragile to him. Will's need to protect and possess grew stronger.

Sounds were crisper.

Smells were stronger.

Everything became that much more.

His lips brushed against bare skin. Even flavors were more vibrant, and the air around them vibrated. He would compare it to the exact moment when an electrical current merged with his body.

This connection grew effervescent in his bloodstream.

How can someone simultaneously make me extra sensitive to everything around me and comfortable in my skin? Will asked himself.

"Hey, is there any more of the-?" Jeff suddenly stopped. "Oh, sorry, I'll-"

"No!" Allison said, jumping away.

She rushedly spoke, not making eye contact with either man, "Jeff, there's plenty left. Will, help yourself to the stew. Oh, and a sandwich is in the refrigerator." Allison gestured toward the library. "Can I pick up those files on the table in the study?"

"They're ready. I'll be there in a few," Will replied.

Allison paused, stole a glance at Jeff, and then switched back to Will.

He remained at the stove, facing Jeff with thumbs hooked into the belt loops, rocking back and forth on the balls of his feet. His expression became closed off, but the gaze that locked onto hers burned hot.

A fluttering glance moved around the surrounding area, ensuring it didn't land back on Will. "Okay, I'll wait for you." A grimace flashed across her face when meeting Jeff's amused expression. "Ah. See ya, Jeff."

"Yeah... alright. Ahh, thanks for lunch again. Pete and I appreciated it."

"No trouble. I'm just relieved we are... you know. Good. Um... okay. Later." She missed Will's brief look of resolve while darting away.

But Jeff didn't.

And he edged Will to the side to help himself to a third refill. "Oh well, I was going to call 'heads.' Or, in your coin's case, floating eye and toss for her. But-" he spoke under his breath– just loud enough to be heard.

Will's hands dragged a path through his hair before dropping them to rest on the hips. "Alright, already, just let it go. I'll let you in on it when I figure it out myself." Will laughed without humor.

"Seems like you already did," Jeff said, turning around. His amused smile spread wider. "But you want to fight with yourself a little longer before giving in."

Will just shrugged.

"Hang-loose, big Kahuna. My money's on you."

Will laughed at the whole situation, this time with genuine humor. "Thanks, Jeff. I'll let you know how it's going."

Jeff chuckled. "I think I'll figure it out. Probably better than you."

His focus on Allison's retreating figure caused Will to miss that last part.

"Alright, I prefer the tedious boredom of watching the security cameras to discussing your love life." With his bowl in hand, Jeff's attention flashed from Allison to Will.

A loud door slamming made Jeff wince, but a grin returned soon afterward.

Will's chuckle, this time, sounded dark, definitely not PG-rated. With a certain spitfire behind closed doors, the upcoming verbal sparring had anticipation strumming in his blood before his friend's comment fully sunk in. A glance in Jeff's direction accompanied the reply, "Yeah, right! I'm sure the abundant selection of cable channels available doesn't hurt either."

"Oh- Go to hell, you Ankle-snapper," Jeff spoke with a good-natured, relaxed reply consistent with their typical banter. "See ya, *BARNEY*," he called out, swaggering back to the control room.

In surfer lingo, Barney meant a beginner, not knowing how to surf. Jeff used it often enough and others like it that Will had bought a surfer's lingo dictionary years ago. Someone had to understand and lend translations for the team.

Usually, Jeff never referred to Will by that name, but in this case, he suspected Jeff might be right in the dealings with managing this situation.

However, Ankle snapper, concerning himself, Will would need to look up before agreeing or disagreeing. But finding a spare minute to put toward that research fell far down on the list of things to do.

And Will could think of one or two more enjoyable items–all with a particular person taking center stage–spurring him on.

His computer-like mind recognized an opportunity when presented, and he began strategizing the chess pieces accordingly. And because of that, Allison had only a short wait before Will came striding into the office.

Retrieving the stack of folders on the conference table, he distractedly scanned through them. "With the tight security here and knowing you are quite safe; I reconsidered an earlier decision. "The files got stacked together, making a repetitive tapping noise while hitting the wood's top surface. "I thought you might want to review files on the investigation and give us a hand."

"Oh." A short, puffed-out response hastily followed, "sure."

Allison's fleeting hope that Will was relocating back to DC quickly died. After damp palms smoothed the fabric crease along her lap, she rose from leaning on the desk. Their fingers touched when she reached out to take the folders.

An electric tingle zinged up her arm.

She pulled away, stepped backward, and stumbled into one of the chairs. The heavy, wood and leather-upholstered piece got knocked over and hit the floor with a resounding thud.

Although not her most graceful moment, Allison didn't care. Any diversion became necessary to settle her pulse as she put the files on the nearest surface and went for the chair.

Will quickly intercepted.

"Don't worry," he said and caught her against him. Adjusting the hold, he kept one arm tightly encompassing her waist as the other arm reached to grab the chair. By doing that, he had her arching back as he leaned over.

The jarring movement released Allison's hair from the loose bun to tumble downward, streaming past her shoulders in bewitching disarray. The resin sticks fell to the carpet. Their deep red shape got lost in the accent pattern of the Oriental rug.

Instinctively, her arms wrapped around his neck. Which, of course, corralled her in much closer.

Will combed through her thick tresses of loosely curled locks, enjoying the feel of the heavy, silky strands in his hands. As she relaxed further into his embrace, he swept her hair to one side and leaned forward to whisper in her ear.

"I love how your hair feels," he admitted while finger-combing through the luxurious waves. "Don't ever get it cut."

Allison snorted. Angling her chin up, she peered curiously at him. "Like I'm going to listen to whatever you have to say about it." With this close proximity, she found it hard to speak in a normal voice and nearly cringed when hearing her breathy tone.

"Well..." Will said while gathering the strains of silken threads together. Wrapping his one hand around the long locks, he gave a firm tug.

Her head fell to one side, unable to move it back due to his tight hold.

"I'll take advantage now and do this." He ran his tongue across the susceptible spot in the curve of her neck.

Breathless, she could only respond with a shudder.

"And do this-" He furthered his point again by using the hold on her hair to manipulate her body where he wanted her to be. His focus never wavered off her gleaming locks while lowering her down to his lap.

Maneuvering her closer, he moved to occupy the nearby chair.

With her body positioned where it suited him and his attention veering off where her hair settled down beyond his tethered hold, he stroked her exposed skin with his free hand.

He lost sight of the passing of time, enjoying the process of proving a point as his possessive grasp allowed him to control the angle of her mouth for him to kiss. Her delectable taste spurred him on to take more. The need to sate this thirst only grew stronger as he gave in to his desires.

But he reluctantly lifted his head away from her swollen lips when requiring air to breathe again.

Addictive sensations rushed through her body. Allison slowly opened her heavy-lidded eyes to see what he would do next, wanting him to take her back to the swirling pleasures of their combined passions.

Will's face hovered nearer as a kiss landed on her nose. "Now, you know why I love your long hair."

A smile of concession slowly formed on Allison's lips, but her hands clasped a tight hold on his shorter hairstyle, bringing his face closer. "It works the same on short cuts too."

"So it does," Will softly admitted.

She held him to her and claimed a kiss, setting off another round of them, proving their respective points.

Will whispered what he wanted to do to her while his teeth nipped at her ear lobe. He told her in rough-spoken words, in unarticulated sounds, and telling touches how much he wanted her in his bed. Confessing some of the fantasies he desired to make real.

Every touch he gave her, she reciprocated with reckless abandonment. Rocking against his engorged member, stroking their cravings to a roaring heated flame that was sure to burn them both.

But she didn't seem to care.

Her body wanted to reach that peak of passion with him. Only him.

The buzz of the desk's intercom broke them both apart.

Jeff's voice sounded loud and clear, coming from the device. "Will, Frank Marshall wants a conference call with the both of us. I'm ready when you are."

"Give me a minute." Will's request sounded winded.

"Call me when you are ready," Jeff replied before breaking off the connection.

Clear of the passion-induced fog that coated her brain, Allison jumped away, trying to slow her racing heartbeat. Her hands rushed up to press up against her heated cheeks.

Although mentally thankful for the interruption, her body's response wasn't falling in line.

Will slowly stood, shifting his stance to settle the throbbing bulge in his pants while his breath sawed in and out rapidly.

She tried to step around him, squeezing by the vacated chair, tilting the piece of furniture precariously on its side legs.

His position near the table still blocked her from putting more distance between them.

"Careful," he chuckled. "You don't want to knock the chair over again."

Another tide of heat spread across her face and neck. However, this time, it bloomed for an entirely different reason. "Then step away from me," she said through clenched teeth.

A hesitation lasted for just a second or two before he slowly backed away, never breaking eye contact.

Silence prevailed over the room as each plotted their battle plan before Will abruptly spoke. "I have this meeting to take. Why don't you take the files and read them over?" Will eased away, heading for the desk. He grabbed the phone receiver and waited for her response.

When none followed, a smile appeared on his face, like someone who had a secret figured out but had no intention of sharing it. Instead, he gestured to the files discarded on the table using the phone receiver. "We'll meet up later this afternoon after you read those."

Tilting a chin up, quickly swiping up the folders, Allison proceeded out the door in a hasty retreat. "We'll see," got called out before the door slammed shut.

As the heavy-sounding stomps faded away the further she got from him, Will had to agree. "We'll see, indeed," he said, aiming to provide a lot of face time between them in the following days.

Chapter Fourteen

The flashing light on the office phone proceeded with the closing of a door. When the call got patched, Edward Sharpe sent Jennifer Daniels along on an early lunch break.

Edward glanced over to the lounge area.

MJ's taste still hadn't been fully purged from the room. The flashy display of deep cushions and bold printed fabrics offended his sensibilities. But then he spotted Nancy Johnson applying a coat of glossy red substance along those luscious lips, and everything else faded away.

The smell of cherries drifted across the space and messed with his focus. It became tough to concentrate when the thoughts of sexual activities pressed to the surface.

Having her meet in this office had been a big mistake that Sharpe would never admit to making.

"Darling put him on speaker," she purred in that voice that made men crazy with want.

"Don't speak. Just listen." Putting a leash on her impulses had proved impossible in the past, but he still needed to try.

When he paused to activate the call, Nancy pouted and then nodded.

Edward pressed the extension down and sat back in the recently delivered plush leather desk chair. The executive model had all the bells and whistles.

"Campbell, Ms. Buchanan is MIA. What are we doing to rectify this oversight?" Sharpe's greeting sounded more like a demand than a question.

"Maxwell has taken her off-grid. There was no movement on any of the bugs we planted. I'm trying to get more information on the extended family. Maybe they know something," Sharpe's associate replied in a strained tone.

"Forget that. We are pulling on that string." Edward drummed his fingers on the desktop. His gaze darted to Nancy when her hand rose and twirled in a circular motion. "Hold on for one minute." Sharpe barked into the phone and muted the call.

"What?" he asked abruptly.

"If I know anything, it's how that bitch will act. I'd get a team of our guys to watch small private airports around the area where the family is vacationing. I bet she heads there to meet up with them. Or maybe Maxwell will bring her there under escort.

"Either way, it gives us the opening we were looking for," Nancy assured him.

Sharpe nodded once and pushed the button to continue the call. "I want to know what Maxwell has up his sleeve in Florida. I have two contacts that I want you to coordinate with down there. I'll have them call using the code phrase assigned this week. Get them to keep their eyes and ears open for incoming or outgoing movements. Let's keep a small team there ready to intercept."

A slight pause took place.

Sharpe flipped open the file on the desk before adding, "Also, send my assistant an update on the larceny investigation. I need to pick up some hot items for my collection. I don't want the Feds breathing down my neck."

"Yes, Sir." Campbell cleared his throat and added, "Do you have an update on my sister?"

"You should be getting a letter from her shortly. Maybe we can swing a visit soon." His gaze landed on Nancy when she shook her head from side to side. Sharpe's head tilted to one side as his gaze narrowed on her.

Nancy sighed loudly and then jumped in, "Campbell, I'm afraid a visit will not be possible in the next coming weeks.

"Your sister hasn't been the most graceful guest, and I'm afraid she took a nasty fall. There is no cause for concern. I'm sure the break will heal in no time. She needs to stay off the leg and recuperate."

A long pause followed before the caller spoke.

"Then the letter will do," he carefully said. A slight cough escaped before he continued in a more assertive tone. "I'll keep an eye out for the contact information and follow through as ordered. I'm running into a meeting. I can be available for a follow-up call later today."

"Understood. You've been most helpful." Sharpe ended the call and placed the receiver on the phone's base.

Standing, leaning down on the desk's surface, his weight shifted forward. "Why wasn't I notified of Alice Campbell's injury?"

"It just happened. I only know because I had to visit someone at the Freedom Site and heard the news from the doctor on staff. I'm sure you will be getting a report from that timid mouse of yours when she scurries back."

Nancy slinked off the sofa's arm. She led with her breasts with a chin up, shoulders back, and arms swinging loosely back and forth. Womanly curved hips swiveled from side to side on her tall figure.

She made getting from one point to the next look like a Victoria's Secret model strutting down the catwalk. However, carrying a pitchfork while wearing red horns and a devil's tail seemed a better fit for her than angel's wings.

Her posturing by the desk–leaning across it–took care to reveal the purple-laced bra. The ample curves enhanced and pushed out from the clever lingerie that allowed eager eyes to ogle.

"Why don't we close shop early and-" A tongue poked out of her mouth and caressed the rounded contours of her lips.

Sharpe's gaze followed the glistening trail before returning to her exposed cleavage. "That, I can do." He cleared his throat while closing the folder on his desk and straightened the odds and ends on the top's surface.

Pushing off the horizontal veneer, he made his way around, stopping a breath away from her voluptuous form. A hand grabbed her chin and tugged her forward to fall into him.

His kiss claimed a prize, knowing others were equally rewarded. It didn't matter. He had what she wanted. Or, more like, he would have it very soon. Then, he would have to ensure that the following incentive became equally enticing.

He didn't mind sharing.

But he did mind getting the tail end of the leftovers.

He pushed her off him and rearranged his suit jacket. "Why don't you go powder your nose... and put another coat of that gloss on? I'll leave a note for Daniels and meet you downstairs."

Nancy shrugged as her eyes trailed down his body and stopped at the prominent bulge in his pants. She made sure to turn away before the smirk appeared across her face.

Taking advantage of having the office to himself after Nancy sauntered out, he made a quick call. The call got picked up on the first ring.

"Sir?"

"I need you to meet me at our usual haunt." His hand took out the handkerchief in the breast pocket of his coat. A quick swipe took the remains of Nancy's kiss away. "I wouldn't be alone, so be careful how you get my attention."

"Understood. How soon?"

"Make it an hour from now." Sharpe pulled a notepad from the top drawer. The quickly scrawled penmanship made pointed notes of what he expected to finish by the day's end. He would come in early tomorrow to see if it got done to his specifications.

Or else...

A snicker burst from Nancy's lips when the meek and mild nobody who served as Sharpe's assistant hurried back to the office. She smirked when the young woman swiftly looked down to the floor when they passed, careful to avoid clashing glances.

Nancy had no respect for a woman that blended in so well with the dreary walls around them. Pushing into the lady's room, she called out to see if anyone else remained within. When no voices sounded back, and the two stalls got checked, she returned to the door and flipped the lock.

Her phone got pulled from a small, handheld purse.

She never liked carrying anything that could be used against her as a weapon. Although careful not to keep contacts listed, the people she worked for had ways of finding out. So, she took added precautions.

The burner phone helped her cause. Pressing the keys down to the number known by heart, she waited for the connection to pick up.

"Hello?" the person on the other end sounded like he just had woken up.

"Darling, I'm in the area and thought we could meet for drinks." She leaned over the counter and took the wand from a transparent tube filled with red liquid. She looked at her reflection while applying the gloss to her plump lips.

The lips curved in a 'cat got the canary' smile.

Intensely proud of the only procedure she ever had done, Nancy doted on them excessively. They were, of course, an essential tool.

What man could resist looking at them and not imagine them wrapped intimately around their cock? In her way of thinking, not many could, which gave her the advantage.

Nancy often believed that the little head between men's legs made their minds so damn easy to be led around.

"Yes... Great! That place." The voice spoke of his easy surrender, and Nancy's eyes rolled with his reply.

"Hm, hmmm," the purr of pleasure sounded through the device when the caller reacted the way she wanted. "It is close to our favorite hotel." A flicked wrist sent the applicator back into the tube, and she quickly tossed the makeup into the purse.

A pair of light blue eyes rose and met the reflection in the mirror while she adjusted a strand of burgundy-colored hair back in place. A nod and smile were reflected through the glass.

This arrangement would better suit the goal than Sharpe's lame idea.

"Yes, my sweet. I can't wait to see you too. I'm counting the hours until I'm in your arms again." Nancy grinned with malice.

Her thoughts of men often spiraled around stupidity.

Well... all except one.

William Maxwell became her exception to the rule.

Chapter Fifteen

A couple of days had passed, and the two ex-lovers, tucked away in hiding, remained in a shaky truce. Allison and Will's interactions mostly revolved around getting updates on the investigation and occasionally around lunch or dinners.

What kind of interactions resulted in their time together became anyone's guess.

Most of them brimmed with sexual tension and suggestive banter–primarily by Will. During other times, they strived for a distracted and aloof manner, but that rarely happened. Each demeanor provided a reactive response from the opposite counterpart, leading to heated discussions. And a running bet–instigated by Jeff–between the security personnel gave them all an invested interest in each exchange.

It seemed that Will took great pleasure in keeping Allison on her toes. At the same time, Jeff became the neutral party that provided a buffer between the combative and tense-ridden atmosphere whenever the ex-lovers shared the same space for more than a few minutes. Because of this, he also relayed information between them when avoidance became their fallback strategy.

So, when Will had assembled yet another ample pile of files to look through, she hadn't thought anything of it. Other than their usual subsequent stress-filled get-together that would follow afterward.

But this time, their meeting could become so much more.

Allison didn't know how to avoid the discussion that would likely follow. And an hour later she was pacing inside the four walls of her bedroom.

Will's strategy of changing tactics and shifting moods had her constantly second-guessing everything. She figured it was an FBI trick to keep a suspect on the defensive, so a mistake became likely.

And boy is it working.

Stopping at a window, Allison brushed the curtain aside.

Not that I'm a suspect.

The spacious view of the pool and adjacent gardens below went unnoticed. Their vivid colors and impressive details of both man-made and nature's components creating a spectacular outdoor space were overlooked over an inner, heated debate.

You should tell him. Allison argued with her conscience like an imaginary angel resting on her right shoulder.

No, too much has happened.

That other–not-really there–voice argued from the opposite shoulder. Allison could only imagine that the angel's head shook in disapproval with the opposing team's input.

Her nervous movement quickly returned as one critical point kept circling.

There were pictures–lots and lots of pictures.

And somebody filled all those images with her as the main subject: going to work, getting mail at home, jogging at the park, and socializing at a bar with Jake and Debbie.

Even a few got taken while she had been out on a date.

A work date–mind you–but a date nonetheless. Her angelic mindset formed that distinction.

The not-so-angelic voice huffed out in outrage. *Life with friends and family is not a part of the FBI's investigation!*

By looking at all the information provided, it surely seemed so.

She would have suspected Senator Buchanan's hand in this setup if she hadn't just read the other files regarding the thieves and the other disturbing circumstances having nothing to do with her life.

He would jump at the chance to sweep her back into the fold.

It wouldn't matter either way if this whole situation blew up on her now.

Allison collapsed on the nearby bed.

Will must have already seen the reports, having been the one to gather them up for her. She couldn't understand why he would disclose these reports centered around her.

Was he testing me?

Did he reveal any clues as to whether he suspected anything or not?

Resting on the edge of the bed, defeat made her head bow and her shoulders droop.

Allison groaned. She pulled the ornamental hair sticks from the loose bun. Shaking out her hair, loosening some of the tightness around the shoulders, she strived for calmness.

Even knowing Will well enough that something would have been said by now, Allison's heart rate continued to beat rapidly. A rhythm pounding like a steel drum. It felt constricted in her chest.

Just a matter of time before he or someone else in the investigation finds out.

Add in the irrefutable aspect that falling back into a physical relationship with him came uncomfortably close each time they were left alone together. If they succumbed to this crazy attraction, and she didn't tell him, Will would never forgive her.

And he had the resources to make her life a living hell.

Did we take adequate steps to cover this up under this kind of scrutiny?

Her thoughts circled. The tight squeeze of her fingers pressed against her forehead did little to hold back the bubbling panic. Worse came the consideration of Allison's uncle deciding to take a more in-depth look because of this mess.

She jumped up and headed over to the piles of paper on the settee. But the agency didn't dig far enough.

Yet. A poor, defenseless piece of furniture got kicked in the leg.

Its unwarranted abuse caused the piles of files to fall like a small paper avalanche. Allison bent down, hurriedly attempting to place them back in order, and hesitated when spotting one particular photo.

Studying the image carefully, that memory of the playground came back in perfect clarity.

The picture caught the blur of leaves kicked up by early spring's roaring winds dancing around them. Sara had been on a swing with Allison tying Sara's shoelaces.

They had been laughing at a knock-knock joke that Allison had just finished telling.

A photo perfectly captured that joyous moment in time. The intense connection that Allison and Sara had for each other stayed crystal clear for all to see.

God, how can he not know? Allison reasoned while slowly laying the picture down on the table.

It would be crazy to stay.

Worst-case scenario, she could go to her uncle. She gathered the other images and fallen pages and efficiently filed them back into their correct folders.

As a high-ranking political figure, Senator Buchanan had the means to keep Sara safe from this deadly organization. Even though that protection became equally controlling and evasive, it would have to do until she figured something else out.

Allison hesitated in returning the precious photo to the correct file. Unable to let the picture go, she folded the image and tucked it into the sweater's side pocket.

While placing the folders on the coffee table, her head shook in regret. Will would eventually connect the dots. Or she could let it slip in a passing thought.

Distance.

Getting distance seemed the only way around this.

"Maybe, once we are all free of this present threat-" Allison sighed before adding, "Maybe by then, I'll have a solution."

One thing became clear.

It wouldn't be right to keep her sister and Peg's husband, Bob, tangled in this situation even though they would most likely argue against using Senator Buchanan's help.

Allison also saw no sense in having them put their lives on hold. Although selfishly, she wanted to keep things the way they were.

But hadn't the investigation taken several years already? How much longer before it is finished?

The angelic voice whispered, *Yeah, you need them to help cover your lies for a little longer.* The disapproval coated every corner of her mind.

Not to mention knowing what you are really running from.

Her eyes squeezed closed as her head shook from side to side, wanting to deny the truth. But staying on the perimeter of Sara's life, seeing her growing up safe and happy, had worked better than not seeing her at all.

But she did let go of Will. And made sure he stayed away. Knowing how increasingly hard it had become, her resolve faltered, wanting to give in.

To have Will in her life. To have her family together was everything she wished for. But the fear of her family's curse striking again prevented her from moving forward. Plus, the world in which Will operated, a world where he and others held incredible powers, risked even more than most, and the chances became increasingly higher.

Her heart rapidly thumped, knowing the risk of claiming Sara. Allison sighed again in defeat.

Everything had become such a mess.

Go get my daughter and disappear, her mind rationalized. And then contact the authorities only after her uncle took them in.

Maybe she could give herself a small reprieve while allowing Sara time to adjust.

Before I vanish from their lives.

A soft knock on Allison's door jolted those dark thoughts away.

"Come in!" Allison called out. Expecting Will's entrance, she took a deep breath and started a verse of Mother Goose.

The door opened inward and stopped halfway.

Jeff poked a head through the small opening as she slowly approached the door. His smile appeared sheepish, but the eyes brightly twinkled. "Hi, pretty lady. Want to go out and get some fresh air?"

The unmoving air in her lungs got expelled. "Why? Is it time for all the inmates to walk the courtyard?"

Jeff's grin immediately died.

"I'm sorry, Jeff," Allison said softly, swiftly adding, "It was just a joke. A real bad one."

She reached out and gently patted a cheek. "Besides" Her eyes mischievously danced. "I would have to be crazy to want to leave all these hunky and handsome bodyguards."

"What about Will? Would a girl want to leave his company, too?" Jeff grinned with wicked amusement.

"I refuse to respond to that comment." Allison pulled the door all the way open.

"Listen," Jeff said while stepping inside. "Will asked me to go into town to drop off a package. I was going to stop at a fast-food place and get burgers for everyone. Want to come?"

Before she could answer, he added, "Will suggested you might want to get out."

"Oh."

They didn't know the half of it. Allison excitably thought before saying to him, "I could do with getting some air."

Startled, she jumped when something soft brushed her thigh and braved a look downward.

Jeff raised a handled canvas bag that had missed her attention earlier. "We both feel it's safe," he explained. "But, if you don't mind, I want you to take some additional precautions."

"Sure." Allison looked inside the bag and then headed for the bathroom. She paused and swung around. "Do you know where my purse got to?"

His expression turned sheepish again. "I do.

"Will left it behind.

"He got overly cautious regarding bugs and tracking transmitters. He has your wallet, phone, cash, credit cards, and other stuff. Before you even ask, he said to tell you no. It's not a good idea to use your credit cards or phone. They could track your whereabouts when used."

That no good control freak can just-

Allison's jaw clenched. She could have easily wrung Will's neck.

"Oh." She inwardly cringed. The ability to speak in complete sentences short-circuited. No identification. No bank card or checkbook meant no access to cash.

Making it nearly impossible to get out of here.

A smile wobbled a bit, but she shrugged and said, "Okay, I guess you're buying then?"

He quickly nodded back.

In truth, withholding their personal effects if the sweep had cleared them wasn't a part of the agency's procedure. Personally, Jeff understood why his friend behaved like a Neanderthal.

But did that excuse Will from making a big mistake?

"Let me go change." Allison walked past him to get to the bathroom.

Pulling out the first item in the bag, she shook out a wig and studied the thing. This whole experience got surreal for her. Never in a million years would she have guessed she'd be doing this sort of thing.

Unless for a costume party or another Halloween Gala. But she gave those up after breaking things off with Will.

A lot of bad memories.

It took a few minutes to secure the bobbed-cut hairstyle and make the wig look natural. And she laughed at the person reflected back. The wig's length swayed just above the shoulders when shaking her head from side to side.

She bent down and checked the bag for anything else. There was just one item remaining, and when putting it on, she fussed with the oversized, black-framed glasses obscuring most of her face.

After a final look at the stranger in the mirror, she exited the bathroom and met Jeff by the door.

He studied the disguise and nodded in approval. A grin appeared when Allison did a quick spin to show off the new look. "You make a good blonde."

Allison laughed and looped their arms. "Let's break out of this joint and get some greasy burgers."

Jeff chuckled and tugged playfully on their linked hold as they exited the room. As they made their way down the hall and toward the stairs, Jeff teased Allison with some dumb blonde jokes.

This had Allison's laughter echoing in the stairwell the whole way down. But at the back of her mind, other concerns poked through.

What she had to do wasn't a laughing matter.

Chapter Sixteen

Jeff led Allison through familiar rooms on the first floor until passing beyond the kitchen. She would have liked to peek inside the several door openings along the hallway, but their determined pace gave her no opportunity to linger.

They stopped at a doorway to the left where the hallway dead-ended into another lounge area. Allison noted that the house had quite a variety of rooms to hang out in.

Punching in a code by the door, Jeff disengaged the lock and gestured for Allison to proceed ahead. Another code got punched in when the door closed behind them.

Easing around, she stood facing three identical vehicles. All of the Ford Broncos had a dark grey color and nondescript features.

I'm not sure how anyone can tell them apart.

The only noticeable detail about any of them became the dark, reflective glass windows.

Jeff walked confidently to one of the vehicles. "I'm assigned to the middle one." He pointed to the garage doors, banking the exterior wall.

"Are you telepathic like Will? I was just thinking that." Allison's thoughts screamed in panic while heading toward the passenger side.

The unlock mechanism clicked, and she opened the door. A struggle to get up and into the seat while using the inside door handle took a few moments. A heavily sounding sigh escaped her parted lips.

"Sorry," he said, chuckling over Allison's height-challenging predicament.

"No, you're not," she said while laughing back.

His mischievous smile grew wider as he reached for his seatbelt. After snapping it in place, he pressed the ignition control and started the engine.

Allison, with a resonating click, followed suit with her seatbelt.

Jeff reached up to hit the garage door's remote. "I'm a low-ranged telepathic like Will," he explained as the center door quietly opened. "My dominant talent is telekinesis. But I can't connect with you telepathically."

Their gazes briefly met before a grin flashed, and he twisted back to face the front. "But your facial expressions are animated and very easy to read."

Her returning grin slightly trembled. It took everything she had to try to look straight ahead and relax.

After a few minutes of maneuvering through several side roads on the estate's property, he slowed down and stopped at a large wrought iron gate encompassed by high stone walls.

A button on another remote device tucked above her visor got pushed. The gate slid sideways, providing an opening. The paved road continued shortly past the gate, and as they passed through, Jeff pushed the device again, letting the gate close behind them.

"You seemed surprised that I couldn't read you?" Jeff glanced her way before returning his attention back to the road. They had reached a public highway a quarter of a mile past the front gate.

However, it wasn't much of a road.

The estate's roads were pristine asphalt compared to the one they were presently riding on. The vehicle bounced over gravel-covered asphalt, and multiple large craters scattered throughout.

"I was- I thought because Will could read my mind so easily, it must have to do with my lack of shields," Allison chose to answer honestly.

"That could be more about your connection to each other than anything else."

"How can you tell? Especially since I don't possess any strong talent." She sighed.

"Oh, if you didn't have strong shields, I could penetrate your mind. Even though telepathy isn't my greatest ability, I'm still reasonably strong."

"What town are we in?" Allison asked. While Jeff darted a look to the passenger's side, she continued staring out the side window. A pensive expression was mirrored in the window's reflection.

Will had often suspected that Allison, too, possessed special abilities, which he theorized on multiple occasions in their past. But they never could identify a specific talent.

"You don't believe me. Why?"

"I would have seen it by now," Allison softly replied. Her head swung around, and her eyes met his.

"Some strong talents lay dormant for years."

"For twenty-eight years? I don't think so." Allison swiveled back toward the side window.

Jeff tilted his head from side to side. "I'm not so sure." He tapped his fingers along the surface of the steering wheel. "Ah, Will mentioned that you didn't take it well when he told you about his gifts.

"Do you still feel the same way? It could be that your aversion to these...abilities has blocked-"

"No. I don't have an aversion to anyone with these gifts," Allison admitted in a rush of emotion, interrupting Jeff. "It just took me some time to wrap my head around it. And I don't want the complications that arise from knowing about them, is all," she confessed softly before adding a stronger voice, "So, what town are we going to?"

He took the hint and let the subject drop. "Westwood, West Virginia."

Her mouth remained wide open for several moments. She hadn't realized they had taken her so far from home.

But–not so far from Florida.

"I, um. I had no idea we left the state."

Before returning his consideration to his driving, Jeff stole another glance in her direction. There had to be a reason why Will allowed Guardians, Inc. to take the security detail contracted by Senator Buchanan for Allison's protection. The same protection that had shadowed her without her knowledge and reported back to Will.

Three years ago, Will's declaration of Allison and their ended affair didn't fool him. Unfortunately, Jeff couldn't question any of those details at the time because some family drama of his own had taken him away.

But being around this last year did give Jeff some first-hand insight. So, Will's overly repeated portrayal of their relationship as only being casual didn't hold water. *I'm not the only one to see that these two are fighting against the tides. And we all know they will eventually succumb to the moon's pull.*

Jeff grinned and softly said, "Me thinks the man doth protest too much."

"What?" Allison turned.

His head shook quickly from side to side, shifting to face forward when replying, "Nothing."

After fifteen minutes of flat highway with crisp green fields and horse farms side by side, Jeff's gaze briefly met hers. "Welcome to the small town of Wedgwood, West Virginia, population about eight hundred, give or take."

Allison laughed back in response while adding, "You're kidding? I had more in my graduating class at college."

"Very serious," he replied. "That's why I picked it. It's small, but not so small that we draw attention. No one but Will, myself, and a handful of men know where you are."

Jeff had just stopped at a stop sign. He waved along a blue pickup truck filled with hay to go ahead of him. The old couple smiled in the truck's cab and gave a friendly wave back before pulling forward. After a beaming smile back at the couple, he shifted toward Allison, wearing a severe expression.

"Ashland is twenty-five miles in the opposite direction from the safe house. It's pretty common for residents to come here for the bigger stores. So, we won't bring unwanted interest, but we can keep an eye on other outsiders."

Whistling, he maneuvered into a parking space in front of the town's post office. "Come on. Let me get this package sent out."

"What package?" she asked, and Jeff pulled his leather jacket aside to reveal a small parcel tucked into an inside pocket of his coat. She also noticed the harness and weapon tucked securely in place.

Allison's body jerked. She wore a perfectly formed 'O' on the lips when her gaze jumped to his.

Jeff let the jacket drop back in place. "Don't look so shocked. You're under the best protection that US tax dollars can buy."

His grin, bordering on being cocky, had Allison chuckling. "Oh well, put it that way. I'm in serious trouble then," she teased.

"Fo'Sho Ciara!" he laughed. "You sure know how to hurt-a-fella."

Allison jestingly pushed at him. "What the heck did you call me?"

Playing right along, he tugged and pulled her toward the entrance.

"Fo'Sho means, for sure, and Ciara means beautiful girl." He winked while opening the post office's door.

Allison proceeded him in while a sinking feeling of regret followed in her wake. She liked Jeff a lot and could see them being good friends. But if she did what she wanted to do, this new friendship would be over before it even started.

Chapter Seventeen

The Wedgewood Post Office looked typical for any small town. The old postmaster pretended to be more concerned with the postage weight and supplemental postage cost than the mailer.

After a good ten to fifteen minutes passed, the package–as well as juicy gossip–finally exchanged handlers.

Allison smiled, spotting Jeff's flirtatious wave back to the old but still female–now blushing–postmaster.

The angelic voice sighed in her head.

He is such a nice guy.

Another stab of guilt plunged deeply into Allison's chest as he helped her get back into the vehicle.

Settling in the driver's seat, Jeff twisted to the side. "You okay?" he asked while clicking on the seatbelt.

"Yeah- Why?" Allison breathlessly answered.

"You had a pained look when I got in."

"Oh, well, it's nothing," she said, waving her hand in a simple swiping motion.

"Stomach pains. I'm just hungry," she further explained.

He laughed and started the engine. "Well, let's get you fed, Ciara."

Her best attempt at a sincere smile partnered with a dark thought. More than a stomach ache could be deserved if what she set out to do got accomplished.

Jeff pulled away from the curb, drove a few blocks, and turned into a small place called 'Billy's Fast Eats.'

The small, quaint diner had an outdoor park and serve, plus a drive-thru window that looked like it belonged in the far past. Servers on roller skates streaked back and forth, taking and delivering orders for parked customers. The fifties' vibe played on bright colors, loud music, and quirky, nostalgic details that showcased a fun place to visit.

And by the number of cars in the parking lot, a local's favorite.

"Um... Can we eat in? Then get some take-out to go once we finish? I am starving–besides, I need to use the ladies' room."

"Sure," he replied without hesitating. "I can eat something right now and get something for later." He pulled into an empty parking space on the right, outside corner of the diner, close to the entrance.

Like a bat out of hell, she headed inside.

"Whooa-" Jeff caught up and halted her before opening the entrance door.

"Allison. I need to keep you in a safe spot in case something happens."

She felt like such a jerk. "Oh, sorry, I just have to use the ladies' room."

"Okay," Jeff said with a short chuckle. "What do you want?"

"Uh, yeah. Okay, I'll have a cheeseburger with everything and fries."

"What to drink?" he asked while studying the restaurant's interior.

Reading the menu board, Allison bit her lower lip. "I'll take a chocolate milkshake and water," she said.

"Boy, you are hungry," Jeff teased.

The grin sent back wobbled a bit while she made her way to the restroom. Her hand reached for the spiffy, partial hubcap-turned door pull when Jeff halted her again.

"Let me check it out, Okay?" He pulled open the door and called, "Maintenance!" When no one called out, he went inside and checked each stall. After finding the restroom clear, he said, "Lock the door behind you." Brushing past, he went to get in line.

She nodded while heading inside. The door clicked shut after she cleared its closing path. With shaking hands, the lock was secured.

An advertisement on the order board declared that they made old-fashioned homemade milkshakes.

This gave her a little lee-way.

A relieved exhale escaped her lips when what she had hoped to see came into view. She hurried to the small window near the sinks on the opposite wall from the stalls. Testing the window, she pushed up, opening it without much effort. Carefully climbing up onto the counter, she looked below the window outside. No obstruction blocked it, and luckily, a dumpster with its lid closed was positioned right outside.

Allison solidified the plan while heading to a stall. She needed to use the facility for real if she could pull this off.

Soon enough, exiting, she caught Jeff's eye while he paid for the food. Spotting her gesturing toward a side booth of windows, he gave a negative jerk of his chin and pointed to an inside corner booth instead.

Thumbs went up, and she went to sit down. Hoping to force Jeff away from the front windows, she chose the seat wisely.

Coming near with a loaded tray, Jeff said, "I need to switch sides with you."

"Oh, sure. How about I slide over, and you sit with me?" She moved to accommodate him and helped set the food on the table.

She made a drawn-out production of eating. She moaned in pleasure while drinking the chocolate milkshake and, all the while, keeping an eye on what was happening outside near their truck.

When she shifted and gave Jeff an intense study, he paused after taking another bite of a flamed-broiled burger.

"Whawt?" he said over a mouthful of food.

"Why didn't I ever meet you before?"

Jeff took the time to chew the food. A napkin was picked up from the tray, and he wiped his mouth several times. A darted gaze ferreted out the restaurant before he spoke.

"Will and I were roommates in college, who slowly became friends, and then his family unofficially adopted me.

"My family is very influential. And they were applying a lot of pressure to conform to their traditions.

"My separation from that became short-lived and caught up to me several years ago in a big way. During that time, I told Will and a few others to tell no one of me until I could sort out the mess."

"Is everything okay now?" Allison tenderly touched the sleeve of his jacket.

He took a long pull from his straw before continuing. "Things worked out."

His gaze dropped to the table surface for a short moment and then landed back on her. "I resumed my position with the FBI. Will came to DC with me, and I've been his shadow ever since."

Allison's hand landed on his, and she gently patted him. "I'm glad he has you."

Just then, a rush of customers, both outside and inside, got the place hopping. The half-eaten burger was put down. Her hands settled on her stomach, and she leaned back in the bench seat. "I'm stuffed," she said while watching Jeff unwrap a second burger.

"The take-out window is swamped. Why don't I get back in line and order the rest of the food?" Allison suggested. "You can finish the rest of your meal-" She smirked and pointedly stared as her remaining food got snatched and added to the pile by him. "As well as mine and meet me up there."

"Okay, sounds like a plan." Jeff stood up to let Allison out. He gave a rundown of the team's dinner orders back at the safe house.

Reaching back for the chocolate shake, Allison caught Jeff's amusement and shrugged.

As she had hoped, he flipped to the other side to keep an eye on her. She reached one hand out for money. The hands coated in burger toppings had him gesturing to the wallet placed in the tray.

Taking the wallet and getting in line, she casually took the lid off her shake. As a hand lifted the drink to the mouth–seemingly by accident–she let the chocolate dessert spill on her sweater.

The gesturing to the stain and then pointing to the bathroom did the trick. Jeff smirked and nodded in an affirmative manner. And Allison hurriedly entered the bathroom and locked the door. She rushed to the sink, twisted on the faucet, and checked out the stalls by bending down–looking for feet below the stall doors.

Good to go.

Pulling the sleeve of the stained sweater off, she tossed the discarded apparel on the far side of the counter. Walking around with a big stain on herself would cause too much- unwanted attention, which did not make sense in the whole–sneaking away–scheme of things.

But too focused on getting out, she didn't notice the sweater drop to the floor and the glossy picture falling out of the pocket.

With Jeff's wallet between her teeth, she jumped up and opened the window.

Bringing a leg up, easing it over the sill, and through the opening, she was thankful for the upper arm strength gained in her daily training. Pulling up, using the window's upper trim as an anchor, her other leg came up and cleared the threshold. Her rear end balanced across the sill's trim. While carefully twisting around, she lay across the window jamb with her legs hanging down on the outside.

A tight hold on the windowsill's thick trim allowed her to shimmy further down until her foot–with a barely-there touch–skimmed the dumpster below. A small calming inhale was released before letting go of the window.

The hollow metal thud announced her smooth landing.

She spun around, jumped from the dumpster, and ran back along the diner's sidewall. Easing around the corner, she immediately looked for Jeff.

He still sat, finishing up his meal and clueless about her escape. All she needed was a few more precious minutes before he went to check on her.

As if fate was lending her a helping hand, she eased around to the opposite side of the diner, where a circle of teenagers gathered. And her arrival had come just in time to give a helping hand to one of the young women in the group.

Hopefully, this would get Allison some help in return.

Chapter Eighteen

Meanwhile, back in Washington, DC, in a quaint–but very exclusive–restaurant, Nancy Johnson sat in a booth in the back.

The clientele's attention centered on their companions' hushed conversation more than the menu's fine food. With strategically placed wall sconces and table-lit candles, the low lighting encouraged intimacy and discretion.

Nancy's appearance completely contradicted that notion.

Her whole demeanor shouted–sex.

The ample curves, dressed in tight-fitting, shimmering, flame-colored fabric, with a low dipping neckline and high, ass-skimming hem, made a man want to get a closer look. The long legs adorned by four-inch heels promised a favorable encounter.

If not drawn in by Nancy's appearances and practiced guile, her unique ability–which provided an additional allure–persuaded them otherwise. Only a slight few had immunity to her powers.

Indeed.

None of the men she had encountered during those long-ago stints in foster care had resisted. The husbands, the housemothers' boyfriends, or the foster parents' sons couldn't say no to what she knowingly offered.

Sex could be used to gain power. Anyone who refused to take advantage of that opportunity she labeled a fool.

Nancy didn't see herself as a fool.

She palmed a small compact to check her face in the reflection. An application of glossy amber liquid glided across her lips.

With the arrival of the arranged companion, she released her power and projected the psychic net. It acted as a powerful pheromone, instantly capturing the male's lust. Add in her suggestive body language—which ensured the continuing anticipation—and pleasurable foreplay would remain at the forefront of his mind.

He responded by holding her tightly against him. His kiss became aggressive, possessive, and... Sloppy.

She pulled slightly away to run her long, daringly red-painted nails down his front lapel. "What a welcome home, Darling."

"You look good enough to eat," he said. Catching her hand, he kissed the smooth skin near the pulse point.

His study of her took everything in with intense speculation. "What kind of trouble have you been spreading?"

She pouted. "I'm spreading all kinds of trouble. That's my job, Love."

"Am I just a job then, Sweets?"

"No, you're definitely my pleasure."

His laugh became laced with light skepticism. Even knowing the abundant pleasures came at a steep price, he caved to the promise of sex and power. She and the group she represented were his sources for both.

Coercion was such a powerful tool when used right. Nancy became very good at providing a particular stimulus. Her smugness grew, and she held in a chuckle.

They are all so... photogenic in their release.

Although wives and constituents most likely would disagree.

"Why are we meeting here? I'm getting the impression that I'm just a means to an end."

"Of course, Darling, and what delicious, erotically fulfilling ending is, up... to you. I'm getting shivers just thinking about it."

"Then let's get out of here and go to our favorite room. I made sure it's ready."

Damn- "Business before pleasure."

"Alright. What do we have to talk about?"

Nancy carefully looked around before asking, "How close are you to getting the package?"

"It's hard to find someone who can break into it, and now that I'm not on-site, it's harder to come up with excuses to look around." The man leaned closer and added, "Are you finished accessing the information I already managed to get?"

"Almost. Mr. Sharpe wants access to the newer programs and systems into specific databases, especially the FBI's; we need to know what Frank Marshall knows."

Before the hiring of Will's father, Will's uncle, Vincent Maxwell, had been the former COO. When Vincent had repeatedly hinted at wanting to take ownership of the company, complications arose.

Will hadn't wanted to sell.

So, when his father retired from the political arena, an excellent opportunity to change things around presented itself. James Maxwell's political connections made good business sense for Guardians, Inc.

Or at least that was how Will sold it to his uncle.

Vincent's role shifted to an advisory capacity during the transition. He was also sold a division of dormitory living to take over for a below-market value.

A tokened thank you for all his years of service.

His uncle never indicated having any hard feelings. But in reality, that became far from the truth. And the displaced COO had the power of his shields to keep it well hidden.

"As I told you in the very beginning, your recruit can only hold out against my nephew's powerful ability for a short time.

"Now that I'm no longer in charge, I can't access the new stuff." Vincent drummed his fingers on the table's surface before taking a large sip of his drink.

"They know. We're working on a way to access that resource. We will need you to make contact soon and arrange a meeting. "

"Good luck with that one," he ribbed.

"Oh, I don't need luck. Just be ready to do as I ask."

"Once the package is delivered, when do I get my money?"

"When the job is done to our satisfaction, you'll get what they promised. As long as you don't forget where your loyalty lies."

"Have I given you any reason to doubt my loyalties so far?" Vincent asked.

"No..." Nancy used the tip of her finger to trace along the rim of his drink. Her touch continued and brushed up against his hand, holding the glass while adding, "But when your loyalties get you what you want, it's easy to follow them."

"Good business partners know both sides need to get something out of it to make the deal work."

"So true." She slid out on the other side and walked around the table to lean down to his ear, briefly biting it. "I need to freshen up. Pay for the drinks, and we'll go to that room."

He reached around and skimmed his hand up her dress, liking what he touched. His smile held a carnal promise.

Nancy smiled back.

Knowing his eyes followed her movements, the show became worth the small fortune she was getting paid to string him along.

Such a sucker.

While heading into the restroom, she pushed the speed dial on her cell phone. "Darling. What I don't do for our cause."

"Did he understand the message?" the caller barked.

"Oh, he understood, alright. He's practically salivating for more than just little ole me."

"Good. When will you be back?"

"I have a little errand to finish up, and then I'll come home." She disconnected the call while heading to the large vanity mirror. Tracing the edge of her lips, wiping off any smears, and fluffing up the hair, she prepared to go to work.

Nancy Johnson's best work got done while lying down.

Chapter Nineteen

Back at the hip-hopping diner, a teenage girl had just slipped up and used her incredible ability to manifest fire.

To, of all things, light a cigarette.

And although smoking that young–really any age–was cringe-worthy to Allison, the exposure of the extraordinary gift out in the open would cause the teen some hurt sooner than the smokes.

A young girl walking hand in hand with an adult woman happened to spy on this incredible feat, starting to call attention to that astonishing event.

When, like a shot, Allison inserted herself into the teenagers' circle. Calling out, "Way to go, Stef! That sleight-of-hand trick looks real! You'll be a hit at the talent show next week."

By the expression reflected on the little girl's face, this did what Allison had intended. The little girl–none the wiser–went on her way.

While the teenage girl–looking sheepish and grateful–got a little life lesson regarding the use of her powers in public. With two twenty-dollar bills from Jeff's wallet, Allison also banked on the teen's understanding of fair play.

So, when pointing toward Jeff's Bronco and fabricating a story about a cheating boyfriend, she counted on the teen to return the favor. Especially when further explaining the man's possible adverse reaction to the breakup and the need to leave town seemed like a good idea.

The grateful teenager pointed to her moped and offered a ride anywhere.

Asking about any nearby private airports, Allison's pulse sped up.

And it went even faster when the one girl responded, "Yeah, There's one forty-five minutes away."

Better yet, the group of teenagers agreed to take Allison there.

After explaining the rest of the plan to the gang, they chuckled. And the money Allison offered was declined with a laughing explanation. "Us girls need to stick together."

The teenage boys–wanting to impress their girlfriends–instantly agreed with their part of the ploy. Allison thanked them sincerely, grabbed the helmet the girl's outstretched hand extended to her, and jumped behind the young accomplice.

Allison patted the driver's shoulder, and they were ready to move. The bright blue Honda Moped headed off out of town with a twist of the teen's wrist.

Her mind briefly screeched to a halt when her emotions bubbled to the surface. Even though time spent with Will came with complications, the longing to stay near him tugged at her resolve. She already dreadfully missed him. And learning to live without him all over again would be difficult.

But managing to pull off a quick escape like this wouldn't come again, and she couldn't take the risk of Will discovering the truth.

This, breaking away, she considered the easy part.

The next important step was to catch a plane.

A dip of her head had the dark red helmet briefly resting upon the teen's back when she thought about how that might come about. The acceleration of the moped's movement carried off her heavy sigh with the passing wind.

****

When Allison arrived at the airport, the other steps to land her in Florida were implemented, and the plan quickly came to fruition.

As her knees bounced up and down with nervous energy while waiting for the plane to take off, she felt confident about a successful departure.

But Will was setting plans in motion, too. Just as quickly.

At the safe house, Jeff sat stiffly across from Will as he finished up with some calls. Jeff was trying to understand the cause of Allison taking off in the first place and got distracted from those musings by the slamming down of the phone receiver.

Will's expression turned thunderous.

"That was Debbie; she confirmed our information. Allison got a private plane from an overly thankful client. The flight will arrive at 1900 (7:00 pm) at Sanford International Airport in Orlando.

"The only satisfaction I get from all this is knowing she's terrified right now. Hell, it was one of the reasons I used the drugs. Once laying eyes on our small corporate jet, she'd have fought us tooth and nail."

"If that's true," Jeff interceded. "Why do it like this? Moving them while on vacation would have tipped anyone off if they were being watched. Reading the reports, she would have been aware of this. She has to know her family is safe."

Jeff paused, pulling his fingers through his hair. He frowned and added, "Is she that ill at ease around people with our unique talents? It isn't like we go around using them in plain sight."

"That's not it. Most likely, finding the files on herself got her spooked." Will shook his head at the careless mistake he had made. That file had not been meant for her eyes.

It had been one of the files from his Guardians, Inc. team for him to review before forwarding it to her uncle. And those pictures didn't end up in the report to Senator Buchanan, so Will hadn't really paid attention to the one image.

Until today.

Will's expression was stern and guarded. "She has her reasons."

Abruptly standing, he headed out, briefly stopping at Jeff's side. Will rested a hand on Jeff's shoulder. "I should have known something else was bothering her."

Jeff stood up. "She could be one hell of a field agent. You have to give her that. Hell, those teens were hard to shake."

A distracted shrug became Will's reply.

"Hey... Will." Jeff delayed him from leaving with a light hold on the shoulder. "Care to let me in on what's happening here? I know there's macking between the two of you. But I didn't take Allison to be intimidated by a closeout and do a kickflip. Something's not adding up."

Damn- "You're right, Jeff. It's not that." Will sighed heavily before taking a picture out of his back pocket. The image had been crushed and smudged. The same photo Allison slipped into the pocket of her sweater earlier in the day and found by Jeff on the restroom floor.

Jeff took the picture from Will to get a better look. What he saw looked innocent enough—Allison and her niece.

Nevertheless, the hairs on the back of his neck told him otherwise. He stared more closely at the subjects in the picture. A rush of breath tumbled out, and Jeff met Will's gaze. "Does this mean what I think it means?"

Will nodded in agreement.

"Oh, man, we totally axed! Why didn't we see it before?" He brought a hand up and roughly bore fingers through his hair.

The photo was returned to Will, who jammed it into his pocket that held the gold coin.

"If she would've just remained here as we planned- I would've never guessed. My team got hired by Senator Buchanan months before Sara was born. And Jake and Debbie did mention once in passing that Allison served as a surrogate for her sister. I figured that explained their close relationship."

Jeff nodded. "Allison made an overly exaggerated, irrational move for an Aunt."

"But," Will interrupted. "As a mother, it makes perfect sense."

"What are you going to do?"

Will understood that the question referred to his personal plans, not their case. But it became too long of a list to get into. The hot, aching knot in the pit of his stomach burned like battery acid, eating him from the inside out.

To tightly control this emotion seemed next to impossible.

But he had to if he was to bring them back before Nancy's associates showed up again. And he felt they would be lying in wait to do just that.

That dream of a few days ago, really a nightmare, came to the surface, and he shoved it back down. The thought of Allison being hurt or, worse...killed could put him in a tailspin.

And no way would he let that happen.

"I'm going to get them both. They need to be under tight protection. That hasn't changed."

Jeff nodded in acknowledgment.

His stance shifted, gearing up for movement. He continued, "The plane is ready. Pete's staying behind to follow through on my orders. I'm ready when you are."

Will's hand cupped the photo in his back pocket. His gaze locked with Jeff's before replying, "Copy. Then let's move out."

174

Chapter Twenty

Once Allison had gotten a ride to the airport, the tricky part had come into play. Getting Jake and Debbie's help.

Their conversation hadn't been pleasant.

Allison would have to find a way to make things right with them. She had so much damage to repair when this was finished.

The teens–happy to give their assistance one last time–had lent Allison the use of a cellphone. But having been upset enough to get the message across to her equally frantic friends, Allison had to beg, borrow, and steal to get what she wanted next.

Desperate times had called for drastic measures.

And that drastic measure was Jonathon Hues.

As a repeat client, Allison knew Jonathan wanted more than just a business relationship. Stepping into the plane, she knew it stood the only chance of getting to her family.

Any consequences of accepting Jonathon's help would come later.

Hopefully, much later.

Now–with the loud humming of the plane's motor roaring in her ears–she wished for a handful of anxiety drugs. The aircraft began taxiing toward the runway. With take-off seconds away, she automatically took a sharp inhale and grabbed the armrests.

Watching closely from her post, the private attendant soon realized Allison's aversion to flying.

Haha, aversion–

Allison's ever-present devil's advocate spoke up from the imaginary position on the left shoulder. Today's flight was so much more than mere aversion.

A deathly fear of a fiery ending in a puny metal coffin is more like it.

Her angelic counterpart stayed conveniently absent from Allison's conscience.

The plane's increased acceleration, indicating take-off, had her gripping the armrest like a patient getting a root canal without Novocain.

Before the terrifying experience almost ten years ago, Allison had only a mild aversion to flying. The fact that her guardian didn't prefer that mode of transportation either certainly didn't help.

After all, her mother and stepfather did die in a small plane crash.

But Allison didn't like having that slight fear hanging overhead. So when the chance presented itself, she had begged the Senator to purchase the ticket for a ride at a local Aviation Fair.

On a spring break in college, this seemed safer than what her peers were up to in Miami.

But time had proven her wrong.

On that fateful day, aviation stunts took place at scheduled intervals throughout the day. During one aerial show, a participating plane crashed into its counterpart, and debris flew everywhere.

The smoke had filled the sky as Allison's ride came in for a landing.

A large object had hit the windshield on the passenger side.

She could still recall the impact.

After hitting the windshield, the debris tore along the top of the plane and hit the tail rudder, causing severe damage. Without the vertical stabilizer in the rear, the plane's flight controls had become nearly unresponsive. The sounds of the instrument alarms going off made the dangerous situation even dire.

Due to the pilot's experience, he had kept control of the situation. After clearing the pandemonium below, he had been able to make an emergency crash landing. She had remembered the initial pain of the ground impact, then nothing more.

Allison had awakened in the hospital with her uncle standing by the bed.

His factual, cold voice spoke of the airshow's investigation findings. Someone had sabotaged the other planes, and he suspected their sole purpose was to interfere with Allison's landing. And ever since that day, the strict but affectionate uncle had changed into a very rigid man.

And Allison began to believe in the Buchanan curse.

That's when the aversion to flying became an absolute phobia that she no longer cared to cure. If no car, boat, or train was possible for travel, she took drugs to get on a plane and only huge commercial flights.

Absolutely no small planes.

Today, however, it has become unavoidable. No identification meant no commercial flight.

Funnily enough, once the plane leveled out, the attendant came directly to Allison, offering an alcoholic beverage. "It's on the house," she joked.

Allison grabbed it and inhaled the drink in one continuous swallow.

****

Jeff opened the plane's hatch and called back to Will, "I'll see if they did what I ordered. Meet up with you in a bit." Not waiting for a reply, Jeff jumped down, ran to the outbuilding nearby, and came across an unexpected delay.

Two burly men came out from the hanger with the precise intent to jump him.

Jeff's quick reflexes countered the attack. Luck would have it that the structure's location wasn't in the main public area.

There were no witnesses to catch Jeff using telekinesis out in the open.

Not having the time to spare for capture and detainment, he sent them flying into the lower portion of the hanger's construction, where the build-up from the floor became a concrete block.

The men died on impact.

Jeff drew his gun and clicked off the safety.

Pivoting, he ran back to where Will was taking care of the plane. Two more men stalked near the aircraft. One of them held what looked like a tranquilizer gun.

His reasons for not sending Will a telepathic warning became three-fold. If either man held the same ability, they could pick up the message. Plus, Will's distraction with Allison had put him on edge. No, telling what backlash would ensue. And there wasn't time or enough resources to swipe clean the damage Will's electrical strike could cause.

But when other vehicles arrived on the scene, it cemented Jeff's last reason.

Near the plane's entrance, a man rushed up the retractable steps.

Jeff didn't hesitate.

His powerful energy threw the man hurrying to enter the aircraft into the approaching vehicle. And Jeff went into pursuit mode as the body's impact rocked the leading SUV's frame.

The other intruder spun and ran but didn't get the chance to escape. Jeff, in a flash, came up from behind, around the plane, and wrapped an arm around the stranger's neck. The man struggled violently against Jeff's choke-hold until sagging unconscious. Upon the team leaders' arrival, Jeff dragged the man to the undented vehicle and ordered him to be taken to the nearest field office to be questioned.

Everyone in the vehicles quickly exited. Ready for action.

Their voices carried brisk directives, witnessing observations, counter data from the surrounding details, and relaying multiple communications through their individual devices. Everyone voicing objectives that countered each other.

But a sweeping hand gesture from Jeff interrupted it all.

His sharp demand for updates on Allison's family skirted the incident and served as a pointed reminder that no one wanted to hold up the works and have to answer to Will's ire.

Jeff turned back to the plane when he heard Will's heavy treads making their way down the boarding steps.

Off to the side with the rest of the team, Jeff purposely stayed quiet.

As Will dropped down–making a visual sweep of the plane's exterior around the back–he checked off items on the clipboard in hand. Coming back around, tossing the checklist back inside the cabin doors while passing, he headed toward their group.

That's when the body lying on the ground got his attention. Will swung around to meet his partner's scrutiny. A negative shake of Jeff's head served as a response before focusing on the other men.

Jeff's stern orders put everyone on autopilot. "Shadow. Wizard. Mind the plane. As I'm sure you saw, those junkyard dogs wanted something. See that they're cleared out and relayed to our counterparts here in Florida. Maybe they can find out something about them, but I doubt it.

"This airport is small and well known for its corporate business. But they did come through on our request for privacy. I don't expect any more spit, but tell your teams to be prepared.

"Allison's plane should be landing at Orlando International at 1930 (7:30 pm). Not sure if Hostiles are waiting and watching for her, too. We'll check with the on-site team to see if my assumption is correct."

A loud rumbling sound overhead had everyone looking up. The noise sounded like the sky was falling as a commercial flight came in for its landing on its assigned path, miles adjacent to its location. But it served as a reminder that time actively passed them by while they stood there.

Jeff turned to Will. "Bossman you need to add anything?"

"Yeah, I delayed the landing thanks to a connection, but not for long. I don't want Allison to get suspicious.

"There is no time for dawdling. We'll only beat her by-" His gaze narrowed on his uniquely made timepiece before continuing, "maybe twenty minutes. So, let's get moving. Surfer, which vehicle is ours?"

Wizard threw a set of keys, and Jeff caught them.

Motioning with his head, Jeff pointed toward the vehicle Wizard had exited a few moments earlier and waited for his teammate's nod. Once getting the confirmation–with his left hand in a loose fist, except for the thumb and pinkie held out– Jeff twisted his wrist a few times, sending Wizard a 'shaka' hand sign.

Jeff's trusted team member and friend returned the hand gesture with a thumbs-up reply and then dragged their living prisoner to the other vehicle.

As Will shook hands with the other two men, Jeff added, "Evert, you lead the way. Will and I'll follow. Tell Target he can follow up the rear. Okay. Everyone knows what needs to happen. Let's do a clean wave and get out."

The men went their separate ways and followed the plan.

Everyone knew the stakes they were fighting against.

And that required a speedy extraction.

Chapter Twenty-One

Jeff, his trusted team, and Will left the Kissimmee Gateway Airport as quickly as they arrived.

Will headed toward the passenger's side, so Jeff got into the driver's seat.

A drawn-out squeak proceeded Will's shifting around on the leather seat as they turned onto highway West Vine Street. "Well…" he growled while adjusting and activating the wireless communication earpiece. Something about these attacks didn't sit right with him. "What happened back there?"

At the next stoplight, Jeff twisted in his seat. "Do you really want to go into right now? Or-" Spotting the light turning green, he switched his gaze back to the road. "Or, can we discuss it later?"

He looked steadily at his best friend while Jeff focused on getting to their destination in the most expedient manner. His best friend's mind remained shielded from him. Will couldn't blame Jeff when he, too, was keeping his mental guard up as well.

After a few heartbeats, Will replied, "On the plane." He got back on his cell phone to gather Allison's arrival status.

Fifteen minutes later, steering into the resort, both men stiffened in their seats when picking up a transmitting message through their earpieces. Will swiveled toward Jeff as their guns got pulled from their harnesses. "Don't even think about calling Wizard and his team for backup.

"Keep them on, Allison," he urged before adding, "I'll cover you. Swing around and flank the front entrance."

Jeff hesitated before shaking his head in agreement.

He wasn't happy about it, but they had no time for arguing. "Copy, if we can draw them somewhere remote... Any security cameras that pick us up, you can do your magic and make them disappear," Jeff replied while easing the vehicle into a parking spot off to the side toward the back.

Tapping the security communication device in his ear Will activated the microphone. "Bossman, over. Units three and four span out and get civilians away from the lobby. We can't have witnesses. One and two stay close to the family in their rooms.

"All teams copy."

"Copy" came through on multiple replies.

Jeff and Will's movements became systematically in sync. Jeff's chin jerked toward the one emergency exit on the left.

Will placed a hand on the sidewall. With eyes closing and power reeving-up, Will concentrated and shut down the security program and fire safety alarm. And the nod to his partner had the door click open with Jeff's telekinesis.

Turning to Will, Jeff motioned for him to stay back.

Easing the door open, Will looked around them while the leading agent stealthily moved inside the threshold with a weapon drawn.

Clear, Jeff sent through their telepathic link.

Following him in, Will carefully closed the door behind them. Both security and fire electronics promptly reactivated as he tailed his partner a few feet away.

Their way to the Lobby went uneventful, except for a few excited guests accompanied by Guardians Inc.'s men making their way past them to the emergency exit. The brightness of the Lobby's clerestory skylights with the tall, glass storefront filtered into the hallway ahead.

The two men paused.

Jeff eased back and waved for Will to take the opposite side of the hallway's entrance to the lobby. With a jerk of the chin in the form of a reply, Will eased to the sidewall and peeked around the corner.

The large spanning two-story area stood nearly empty, except for two employees who staffed the front desk and a handful of guests hurrying toward one of the emergency exits on the other side of the space.

"Two of the four intruders neutralized." This transmission was relayed in both men's ear devices.

Nodding to Jeff, Will said softly into the microphone, "Copy. Bossman's eyes on lobby space. Don't see hostiles."

Jeff's gaze followed the progress across the lobby. As the guests rushed through a door opening, their frantic shouts and murmurs came to a sudden halt when the door closed behind their retreating forms.

The sound of something scraping against another surface produced the only warning. Instinctively swinging around, Jeff spotted the two men who had passed them earlier while escorting guests. Both men came up fast with guns drawn and aimed in Jeff and Will's direction.

Will!

That telepathic warning did the trick as Will reacted, pivoted around, and retrieved electrical currents from numerous sources. Multiple streams of energy came rushing to him.

The two men fired tranquilizer rounds.

But none of the flying darts hit their mark.

Jeff swept a hand to the side. The darts–frozen in mid-air– got tossed to the corridor wall to fall harmlessly to the carpet floor after hitting the drywall surface with loud popping noises.

Simultaneously, Will's hands shot out toward the attackers.

Dual streams of electrical current found their targets and eliminated the threat from one heartbeat to the next.

The stillness encompassed the space around them. But the tension in the air made the lack of sound seem loud in their ears.

Uncomfortable.

Will looked down at the two men lying out cold on the floor, searching for any telling clues before the other team members came to the scene. His attention went to Jeff, who immediately began patting down their reclining forms. "My electrical attack will have wiped their phones," Will said softly.

"Yeah, but our guys may be able to salvage them, and you could retrieve the data," Jeff commented as he rolled the closest body over. He looked up and met Will's eyes. "Do you know these men?"

A quick headshake gave a silent reply, but he added, "Not personally, but they've been with my company for over two years. I selected them for the perimeter security."

Jeff switched back to the closest unconscious man. "How far a reach does this organization have?"

Will looked away, surveying the empty lobby. His control on the mounting panic was slipping. How could he keep Allison or his daughter safe when the security breaches kept happening?

A palpable tension radiated from him. They couldn't seem to catch a break, and the constant distractions of putting out fires kept them from gaining ground. Frustration wanted to take over when clear, cold logic was needed. Chasing Allison across several state lines didn't help things either.

His head shook from side to side before his hand combed through his disheveled hair.

"Allison will be here shortly. Let's ensure we get in and out without any more mishaps," he said while turning to Jeff. "Can you make a telepathic perusal of our remaining men? We need to make sure the teams surrounding the family are good."

Sounding like a man carrying the weight of the world, Will sighed. "I'll ensure the teams tiered beyond, get another security sweep as well." His gaze locked with Jeff's while jerking his chin toward the unconscious men. "I grouped them within team four."

****

Close to a half-hour later, tired, strained with tension, and unbelievably hot, Allison entered a sizable, airy lobby–very thankful for working air conditioning.

It was a little after eight in the evening, and she still had much to do. Anyone looking saw a flight attendant done for the day. With brisk, determined strides, she pulled a black-colored flight crew, rolling luggage across the marble floor.

The new wig purchased with the last of Jeff's cash–itched her scalp like crazy.

Jonathan's flight attendant proved to be a female MacGyver. With a few tweaks, safety pins, and tape, Ms. Fessand from Capital Enterprising got the skirt–two sizes too big and tall for Allison's petite stature–to work.

Her walk remained brisk, passing by the front desk. Instead, she headed straight for the main elevators. Casually, she glanced around while a finger repeatedly pressed the elevator call button.

A musical ding announced the cab's arrival, and she hurried inside.

Thankfully alone.

The family's room numbers were relayed earlier when talking to her sister. She hoped to resolve their problematic conversation back at the airport.

Peggy had voiced several concerns in a volume projecting through the receiver loud enough to pull the device further away. That alone–since Allison couldn't recall a time that her sister raised her voice at anyone–made the severity of the situation clear to everyone involved.

But who could blame Peg for stating the obvious?

Sagging against the elevator cab wall, Allison reserved energy as a musical score played through the sound system– reminiscent of 'The Little Mermaid's soundtrack.

The swooshing of the elevator doors landed her on the floor above her sister's room faster than expected. Her hope of regaining any semblance of calm before confronting her sister died with the reflection of herself in the hallway's entry mirror.

Pushing off the wall to rush out, a heavy sigh released from her parted lips.

Running out of time with Will probably close behind; she took the stairs two at a time. The empty bag she carried didn't hinder her. The door to her sister's floor slowly opened, and the cautious pace took her further down the corridor.

A man stood in a relaxed yet ready stance outside a doorway.

Figuring her approach might be okay without shots getting fired. She tugged at the wig while moving closer. Holding a polite smile in place, the wig was removed, and her hair was released from its bun.

Her slim shoulders got raised, and her posture straightened when stopping before the guard. "Hi, I'm Allison Buchanan, and I want to see my sister, please."

He didn't speak, but he did step aside.

The hairs rose on the back of her neck as the handle turned, and she pulled the rolling bag behind her. She stepped into the room.

Seeing it empty, her energy fizzled out. Her slumped frame leaned heavily against the door as it closed.

She carefully released an exhaled breath.

"You look tired, Allison. Why don't you come and sit down?"

A choked cry escaped, and she stood upright, spinning toward that voice.

A bar counter separated the seating area from the kitchenette. A wide column stood adjacent. Big enough to shield a man—even Will's size—from her view.

She stood uncertain, ready to run at a second's notice, watching Will push off from the countertop and straighten to his full height.

"Now, let's not start the chase up again so soon. We have something to discuss first." He advanced to where she remained frozen, never breaking eye contact.

Forgetting to breathe, she saw dots surrounding her vision.

Will's rushed, long strides eliminated the distance between them. The luggage handle got pulled from a limp grasp to be tossed aside. The clasp of a handful of her skirt fabric got her taking in a big gulp of air.

Tugging her along, positioning her further in the room's center, he returned and stood behind the counter.

Allison moved to a set of sliding glass doors and leaned on the cool, transparent panels. The icy temperature of the door's surface helped ease some heat off her body.

"You took quite a chance in coming here."

"I was careful." Her arms got crossed and tucked close to her chest.

"Not as carefully as you think. We had a welcoming party earlier," Will said while rubbing his hands along the fabric of his pants. "My company provides Jake and Debbie's phones. They can't be traced. And the phones you used were too random for them to know about, and therefore, bug. And it was smart to change your appearance after evading Jeff," Will grudgingly admitted. His stance shifted with hands braced upon the countertop as he leaned forward.

"But I knew where you would end up eventually. And someone else also guessed the same thing." Will bounced back to pull something from the back pocket before returning to his earlier pose.

He laid a photo down on the granite surface. "Quite a big risk just to visit your niece."

The same picture she had placed in her pocket earlier held her gaze.

Her breath got caught tight in her chest again.

He knows!

Chapter Twenty-Two

Sara is my daughter, isn't she, Allison?" Will's low voice held a cold fury.

Allison shuddered with the impact of that question.

"Answer me!" Will demanded louder, and Allison's body gave a slight jerk.

Her gaze slowly lifted and clashed with his. "Yes," she whispered.

The secret's burden, kept for so many years, finally came to light. Closing her eyes tightly and holding back the tears, she slowly pushed away from the doors. "I'm sorry to have you find out like this."

"Sorry that it created an additional risk with what's happening. Or sorry that I found out at all?" Will coldly spoke.

She met his stern gaze straight on. "Yes, Will." A puff of air was released and slowly pushed out. "On both accounts," Allison remorsefully said and added in a rush, "Please let me explain." She sat in the chair closest to the glass doors, believing that if things went badly, an escape off the balcony looked possible.

The pool below didn't seem that far, and...

"Try it, and I'll spank your rear end."

Allison jolted.

When silence prevailed too long, he gestured with a sweeping hand motion.

A nod and trembling chin set in motion her effort to explain. "At the time, I thought I was doing what was best for everyone."

Will spoke with a contemptuous look, "Best for you."

Glancing away, she looked through the glass doors instead. "I told you I couldn't have children. Mark wanted to start a family right away when we got married. Finding out the problem was the beginning of the end for my short marriage."

Her shoulders shrugged. "You know what happened next. I wanted to adopt, but Mark had other ideas. During our time together, Will, you spoke of your sacrifices when your fiancé became ill. You were looking for something casual–easy. We both wanted that."

Will remembered that foolish notion. He had also fought hard to believe that lie.

"You think I would compare having a child to a sacrifice? What a small opinion you must have of me," Will interrupted.

"I know you're angry, and you certainly have that right. But if you could just hold off venting, I would really appreciate it. If not, we can just skip this part." She waited in silence for a few moments to pass.

Will nodded once, raising his hands with his palms facing outward, Allison continued, "In the beginning, we both were recovering from past relationships. I didn't expect we'd click so physically and emotionally."

A sad smile appeared on her face as she looked down at her hands. "I began to have strong feelings toward you. At first, I thought you felt the same. At least, physically."

Allison peeked at him. "We still do," she quietly said, looking away again.

"When I thought my feelings only went one way. I got scared. Although we had so many things in common, there were significant differences too."

No way would she disclose her true fears to him.

"I settled in Conshohocken, and you planned on moving to DC to take that contract. You wanted that assignment very much. Plus, it was way too soon for you to be tied into a serious commitment with what you went through with your fiancé, Rachael."

"You assumed wrong, Allison." Will combed his fingers through a head full of already mussed hair. His stubbornness held on tight, not wanting to give her an inch.

Taking a deep breath, she let it out slowly. "I admit I didn't entirely trust you—or my feelings."

Her head tilted to the side. "I didn't handle learning about this secret society of special abilities either. I feared what people could do with those possessing these talents and what others would do to gain control over them. Maybe that is why I doubted our relationship and believed Nancy's lies. Compared to someone holding an incredible gift, I'm rather boring."

She paused, hoping Will would say something. But when nothing followed from him, she spoke in a rushed manner. "At first, when she accused me of being a spoiled rich girl who became the dangling carrot to lore you into my uncle's control, I didn't give it credence. Even if my uncle did introduce us at that Senator's Gala. But when you refused to talk about her... I began having doubts.

"Maybe I was looking for an excuse." She absently plucked at the cording around the armrest of the chair. Knowing Will's penchant for logic, she feared that her family's curse would fall on death's ears. He wouldn't understand the considerable relief she felt after their break-up, believing him safer away from her.

"When I learned about the pregnancy, you had already moved to DC."

"Did you use the pregnancy to get back at what you thought I did with Nancy?" Will fisted his hands, trying to dispel his agitation.

"No! I swear," she assured him. "At first, I didn't believe it. Dealing with our break-up and the complications with my uncle caused a lot of stress. He became-"

Her head shook with the decision to leave out how angry and irrational her uncle had become when discovering their break-up. His fears for Allison's safety started the endless cycle of controlling behavior back up again.

"I had recently reconnected with my half-sister Peggy from my mom and stepfather's marriage. It became everything I hoped for, and my time with her helped in many ways.

"My sister had talked me into leasing her old house since moving in with her new husband. And my condo just reminded me of our time together." Allison's voice trailed off, and a finger traced the fabric's pattern.

Allison looked up and met Will's gaze and then looked away. "Never in a million years did I believe I was pregnant. Hell- my sister bought the pregnancy test. When I took the damn thing, I did it mostly to prove her wrong.

"When it showed positive, I fainted. It scared Peg to death. I came to with her fanning my face with the pregnancy test's paper box." Her hands clenched in her lap, remembering how frantic she had been when realizing the threat her family name could bring to her unborn child. The weeks that followed only made the fear grow to unbearable proportions.

"Later, my sister's doctor confirmed the results. He also told me there were no problems with my reproductive functions other than the slightly tilted ovaries. The regular doctors and specialists I went to convinced me that getting pregnant without fertility methods would be nearly impossible. Mark and I had never conceived-" She shrugged instead of finishing and glanced up at him.

Will's posture remained the same, if not even more rigid. "Where did you find your doctors?" he asked.

"My uncle," she sighed. "The doctor recommended special vitamins for Mark and me that would help with conceiving. We consistently took them every morning with the rest of our vitamins. I later suspected that-"

She absently shook her head. "Well, anyway. When I found out about you and Nancy, I became convinced you two were in a relationship and you never had any real feelings for me. It hurt believing what she said about my uncle's interference could be true."

"Interference?" Will interrupted and immediately regretted it. This definitely wasn't the time to bring up that sensitive topic. "Never mind. We'll get back to that later. Go on."

"Well. Um. I had just started working for Debbie and Jake as a consultant. They have been good friends to me. But at the time, they were better friends with you. I panicked about the pregnancy."

Leaning forward, with elbows resting on her thighs, she massaged her facial features with the open palms of her hands. Her voice softly said, "I didn't want your commitment by obligation. Or mess up your opportunity in DC.

"And there stood a good chance that if I told you what I believed my uncle did." Her gaze locked on Will with an imploring intensity when she added, "You might not believe me. Plus, if my uncle found out, I felt his control over my life would become even more oppressive."

Allison didn't mention that her fear of her family's curse was heavily upon her shoulders.

"So... um, a story got fabricated with my sister's permission. When I discovered I was expecting Peggy and Bob had difficulties conceiving. I told her that I would give my child to them. I told everyone I was a surrogate mother for my sister and her husband."

"God, Allison. You gave away our baby?" Will felt sick inside, wondering if she had such an aversion to the small group of individuals holding these unique talents that she gave up their child.

"No! No. When they laid Sara in my arms, I couldn't let her go. Peggy and Bob assured me they only went along with the story to reassure me.

"I. I couldn't risk my uncle's interference."

Or the family curse touching my daughter.

"So we agreed to follow the original plan, but just publicly. It states on Sara's birth certificate that I was the biological mother by surrogacy. Peggy and Bob are her legal guardians. When Sara tells everyone she has two Mommies, we explain that I am the surrogate Mom, while Peggy is the biological one."

"And I thought how I came to be adopted was complicated. This arrangement certainly tops it," Will said with an edge.

She shrugged again and said, "Sara stays with me often. With my sister and her husband traveling a lot, Sara has a room at my place. She doesn't question the arrangement. It is all she has ever known."

"When Sara turned six months old..." Allison took a deep breath and released the exhale before adding, "I wanted to tell you, but by then, the lie had grown so quickly and affected so many people. I chickened out. The longer it went on, the harder it got to tell."

Allison's attention stayed centered on her lap.

Minutes ticked by in reflection.

Will, more than Allison, needed the time to process everything. His fingers went to the gold coin in his pocket. He brought it out and flicked it between his fingers to manipulate the two sides in a light hold.

The tension settled between them as thick and heavy as a New England's foggy morning. Several passes of the coin's faces flipped around before either one spoke again.

"When I first saw her a little bit ago, I knew Sara was mine."

Allison jumped, startled by the sound of his voice.

"I saw both the shape of your eyes and facial features in her. But she has my coloring, chin, and mouth," Will softly said. "I still can't get over the unique and perfectly meshed features of the two of us in her.

"Hell, she even has my mannerisms, and there's no way she could have picked that up from me because I wasn't around." "Even though Will absentmindedly spoke, Allison flinched with his meaning. "How can anyone looking at her believe she is anyone else's child but ours?"

"People see what they want to see," she softly replied. Her voice got louder when she added, "Besides, Peggy's husband has your coloring and a similar build. And my sister and I look very much alike. No one, myself included, ever thought I could be pregnant, even by artificial means.

"Well, except maybe my uncle."

Moving around the counter, Will leaned on the top's surface. This gave him an unobstructed view through the sliding glass doors, beyond the patio, and down to all the people around the pool. The coin continued to be rolled between his fingers.

The vacationers were enjoying the warm climate. However, some had started to pack it in as the sun had already set. Others gathered around tables, having cocktails, and talking with family or friends.

His focus was drawn to the children frolicking in the water.

He looked below and wondered if his daughter played among them. "Has she shown any signs of having any powers?" he asked and spotted Allison's quick head shake as an answer reflected in the glass. He still couldn't get his mind wrapped around the fact he had a little girl. Would he be a good father?

Suddenly, he pivoted, locked eyes with Allison, and tucked his coin back into his front pocket. A glint flashed in his brown pupils as a glaring message projected into the universe.

A clenched jaw made his lips press tightly together.

Panicking, recognizing that look, she quickly stood to leave. "I'm going to go check on things with... my sister's family. I'll meet up with you in a little bit." If there were a way to reach her family, she would stand a better chance of regaining some control.

"Not so fast," Will softly ordered.

Chapter Twenty-Three

Allison had tried to remain calm. But inside, a heart rapidly hammered in her ribcage. If Will's expression was anything to go by, she wouldn't like what he had to say. "You have every reason to be angry with me. But I just need to go check on-"

She moved–like a bat out of hell–to the suite's entrance door. With a hand on the lever, she pushed down and attempted a quick escape.

But Will got to the exit just as fast.

Leaning heavily on the door, he prevented her from leaving. "You can check on whatever in a minute. We're not done." He took hold of an elbow, escorting her back into the room.

When Will pushed down on her shoulders, she fell into the chair that had been vacated just a moment before. His dominant nature–having taken over since finding her gone–wasn't easing off anytime soon. Moving to sit on the ottoman, he effectively blocked any further escape. "You have a lot to answer for, Allison. But I don't have the luxury to go into it with you now. However-"

He paused and glared at her with a steely resolve before continuing, "I assure you. We will. Right now, I still have a job to do. Your safety is still my responsibility," he informed her.

"No, it isn't. I want someone else assigned to Sara and me," Allison quietly demanded.

Will smiled, but it didn't reflect a friendly nature. "Not going to happen. It will be my job to see that you are safe and ensure the same goes for my daughter."

Her mouth opened to speak.

"Don't talk. Just listen," he demanded. His patience, having expired before she got here, did not look to be returning any time soon. But he did try to reign in the urge to shake some sense into her.

"Now, I call the shots, whether you like it or not."

He leaned in, further intruding upon her personal space. "This is what's going to happen. You will wait here until Sara is brought back up from the pool area. We will tell her about our wedding that will occur-" He paused, looked down at his watch, and added, "in fifteen minutes."

"No!" Allison's head shook in adamant denial. She moved to rise. But Will loomed over her. His presence, so encroaching, had her head resting on the back cushion to get some distance.

"Then... you are going to say goodbye to your family. Let Sara and yourself be escorted downstairs."

His loud inhale through his nose sounded ominous to her, and she geared up for what came next.

"We are all heading back to West Virginia. " He paused to let it all sink in. His frame eased back, arms crossing to rest upon his chest before adding, "You got it, Allison? You're not going anywhere. Doing or deciding anything on your own about my daughter–again."

"You have no authority over Sara and me!" she shouted.

"Yes, I do," he replied in a voice so low that Allison strained to hear it.

Her head continued to shake from side to side while silently shouting; *I will not be forced to do anything!*

But she said, "I was wrong before, and you have every right to have a relationship with your daughter. I want to make it right. I do. But we should ease into it. "

Working herself up into a panic, trying to control her breathing, Allison's choppy response struggled out, "It's going to be quite a shock... When, ah, when we move her away from everything she knows! And, and then, tell her. Oh, by the way, I really am your Mom. And, oh- Here's your real Dad too!"

"Regardless of what you believe at the moment, consider this: You and Sara are in grave danger. I care about that very much. Besides-" Will's gaze darted away only to return and lock onto hers. "Your uncle has been informed and is unhappy with your stunt to get here. He wants to meet Sara."

"You bastard," she whispered, all color draining from her face. It was one thing to know that, eventually, she would have had to reconnect with her uncle for help. But coming face to face with that reality became something else entirely.

"Actually, Allison, I didn't let it slip. And the mistake wasn't done to hurt you."

"Well, it's done, regardless." She tried to reclaim control. "Sara and I will be leaving when he arrives. I have rights. And I don't have to remain with you."

"I can see I will have to do this the hard way." Will pushed the ottoman away, giving them some space between them. With a voice so calm, he agreed, "You're right, Allison. You don't have to go with me."

That immediately made her pulse beat faster. Instinctively knowing she wasn't going to like this next part even more.

She held in a breath of air until he added, "But Sara does."

His tone remained even–not a degree louder than before–but the tick in his jaw showed just how hard it was for him to keep it that way. "I have already received permission from her legal guardians. Sara will remain in my protective custody until I know the threat no longer exists."

"What do you mean? I am Sara's mother! And I'm taking my daughter with me!"

"Yes, Allison, the surrogate mother, but not her legal mother. You gave that right to Peggy," Will explained.

"But I have always been her mother. You know that! Peggy knows that! And she would never go against my wishes."

Will stood up and walked over to the nearby coffee table. Bending down, he opened the file lying on top. He gestured for Allison to approach the file and see what was inside. She slowly came over and looked down at the pages.

The legal document stated that Mr. Robert McNeil and Mrs. Margaret McNeil gave their daughter, Sara Ann McNeil, temporary custodial guardianship to William J. Maxwell IV. Sara Ann McNeil would remain in William J. Maxwell's custody until the duration of a set time: That danger no longer surrounded their daughter, and/or the legal proof of William J. Maxwell IV's parental connection to Sara Ann McNeil was established. DNA parentage testing and/or the legal joint custody was determined between the biological parents, Allison Anne Buchanan's and William J. Maxwell IV's, legal representatives.

He pulled another letter out from the file.

This one, by Will's attorney, requested parental DNA testing for Sara Ann McNeil with consenting permissions attached from Allison's sister and husband for the testing. There was also a document sealed by a judge ordering DNA testing regarding Ms. Allison Anne Buchanan's parentage for Sara Ann McNeil.

Her shaking hand pushed the letters aside, and she moved away. Choosing the lounge chair farthest away from Will, she lowered her trembling frame down to sit. A pair of hands held tightly to her knees helped ease away some of the tremors.

Allison's eyes slowly lifted, and she looked at him.

It became hard to watch as the expressions of confusion and fear played across her face, and Will inwardly cringed. At that instance, he wanted to do so many things.

Hold her.

Ask for her trust.

Give her some assurances and give them time to work it all out.

Even so, his silence remained steadfast, knowing they had to stay with him for at least until the danger passed. He needed to keep them safe. After that, he hoped for the best.

The occasional shouts and laughs from the pool's gatherings below were the only sounds filling the room. It became hard to believe that the normal, carefree lives of others continued while their lives imploded.

Until Allison's soft-spoken voice broke through the stalemate. "So you have temporary custody of Sara until the DNA testing and the parentage is established. How long do you think the testing will take?"

"My connections are reliable. It could happen pretty quickly. Within days, I'm told."

Allison couldn't allow Sara's true parentage to lead back to herself. She skimmed her palms along her skirt's starchy fabric.

"What if we don't marry, don't do the testing, but I agree to go back with Sara? Can I stay there with her for however long this takes?" she asked.

"Yes," Will replied. "Until I'm re-assigned." He cleared his throat before continuing, "I would still do the testing. Sara will move with me, and you will remain in West Virginia."

"So, if I want to remain with Sara, the options are waiting for DNA testing, proving my parental rights-" Allison sighed before continuing, "or getting Peggy and Bill to retract their permission for your temporary custody. Or marrying you temporarily until this assignment is played out, and we clear up our custody agreement for Sara?"

"Those are your choices. But don't count on your sister changing her mind. She's worried about you both and agrees that this is the best thing to do," Will admitted.

"You're something else, Will. You know that?"

"I can certainly see why you might think that. But I'm doing what is best. For you and Sara."

"Yeah, sure. I just love it when someone makes decisions for me and mine and then says it is for my own good," she sneered. Hands clenched in a fist, her angelic conscience emerged and silently added its two cents. *But isn't that what you did to Will and Sara?*

"Yes. That's exactly what you did," Will responded heatedly to Allison's inner thoughts. Even though his tone went softer, it continued menacingly. "Now, I'll give you ten minutes–not one damn minute more–to get yourself together."

Allison's heart would break, but she knew what needed to be done.

"No." She let out a heavy sigh, and her focus dropped to her tightly-fisted hands before continuing, "But I think you should take Sara. Keep our daughter safe until this threat has passed."

She met Will's gaze. "We can figure out custody when all this mess is behind us."

Will's face remained blank, but Allison had shocked the hell out of him.

"If I leave with our daughter, you will never see her again. I'll make sure of it," he threatened in a barely-there voice.

"Ahh!" Allison's distraught cry almost tore Will's heart out of his chest. But he remained fixed on this course.

"You don't understand!" she tried to explain.

"You are right about that! But mark my words. We will discuss this later. Now is not the time. Sara will be sent up with your sister, and if I were you... I would make it go as smoothly as possible. You don't want her scared."

Hearing this, Allison became livid. Her pale complexion immediately went pink. "Damn you! You certainly put me in a position to pave the way for your strong-arm tactics."

Will leaned forward. His lips stopped an inch away from hers. "You haven't seen anything yet, sweetheart. I'll have guards posted outside your door. So don't get any ideas." His hands grabbed her arms, pulling her into him–instantaneously conquering her senses.

The kiss started as a punishment. His teeth nipped her lower lip. When she cried out, it allowed him access to dive in deeper, for the stunt pulled today and what happened in the past.

Her senses spiraled, and a whimper escaped.

Feminine softness yielded to his strength.

His flavors burst on her tongue.

Waiting for the surrender–knowing the exact moment when her hunger awakened–he pulled abruptly away. His fingers and thumbs combed through her locks, grasping a handful of hair and tilting her head to meet his gaze. "You're mine, Allison. I'm not going to let you run away this time."

Again, he landed a brief kiss on her lips before he stood swiftly, spun around, and walked to the door. When pulling it open to leave, he twisted back to study her.

Allison remained on the chair, her face flushed from anger and passion. A couple of fingers rested on her bruised lips, and her eyes were wide open in disbelief. But when they met his gaze, her chin shot out in a show of stubborn defiance, firing off a look of steely promises.

Challenge accepted he pushed back telepathically into Allison's mind. And a grin flashed across his face when her body jolted in surprise. He looked down toward his wrist, calculating the remaining time before returning his gaze back to her. "You have seven minutes," he warned before spinning away.

Striding through the opening, he slammed the door shut behind him. And when a loud crash from inside sounded through the wooden panel, he just laughed and kept moving.

Chapter Twenty-Four

The resounding click of a lamp's switch ricocheted against the bedroom walls. Or at least that was what Miles Jennings thought as he blinked open his eyelids.

Adjusting to the bright sphere anchored next to him, he slowly eased onto his elbows to better face the man stiffly sitting in the bedside chair.

"Sorry to disturb your rest, but I needed to speak with you. I have a meeting and will be gone a few days." Mr. Black tugged on the cuff of his dinner jacket while MJ sat up and leaned against the upholstered headboard.

Although small, the room got done with an abundance of opulent touches. Of course, that shouldn't have surprised MJ when he first awakened in this room a few days ago.

Mr. Black did like having his creature comforts, and these secret basement rooms were no exception.

"No problem, boss. What's up?" MJ rolled his shoulders to ease the stiffness in his upper body.

"How are you feeling?"

"You know how it is," MJ replied while shifting more comfortably on the mattress.

His stomach muscles still pulled and gave him some mild discomfort. "Dying is the easy part. It's the resurrection that kills me." He smirked when delivering the joke.

Mr. Black nodded, but not even a cracked smile altered his neutral expression.

MJ sighed and swung his legs out from under the soft bedding. His feet pressed into the antique rug, and his toes kneaded like a cat against the plush texture of the thick carpet piles. "I'm feeling much better. The shots were easy to heal, but getting tossed around in the water got me banged up.

"Those took longer.

"But, I'm awake more than not now."

His boss nodded again, more than familiar with this agent's unique ability and how sleep played an essential role during the regeneration process.

Having a man who couldn't be killed came in handy.

Black's gaze shifted around the lower level's guest room. "I hope you've been comfortable down here. I wish I could have given you a room with a view."

"It's fine," MJ sighed.

And while Black studied the small room's interior, MJ used the opportunity to do the same to his boss.

Small talk didn't usually fill their time together.

MJ knew how these things worked. Although, at least they remained friendly... ish on the job. That didn't necessarily make them friends.

And this was a bit friendlier than usual, making MJ more than a little nervous.

After all, these many years working together helped form an understanding of sorts. Or one, as well as anyone, could really manage with this enigmatic individual.

Since Black shared so little about his true self with anyone, many were left guessing what he was really about, with the exception of two people.

And MJ wasn't one of those two. "What's up?" he again asked, more than ready for their tete-a-tete to run its course.

This brought Black's attention back to his house guest. He softly cleared his throat and got down to business. "Sharpe is getting settled in his new role quite quickly. He's been busy pulling his people into positions that serve... only him."

MJ nodded and quickly inserted, "I'm not surprised. We knew he was working within the group for his private agenda."

"Yes, well. That was the main reason we gave him more rope." Black's attention focused on MJ's hand that unconsciously rubbed the area where the two bullets entered his body.

The soft, cotton T-shirt hid the healed skin; not even a scar remained of the wounded area.

"With you out of the way, Sharpe will surely hang himself with the leeway afforded with moving up in the organization." Mr. Black traced the seam of his pant leg. His voice sounded bored. "And as you and Michael theorized, his arrogance is a tool we can use. Since I'm... one of his focused interests, we can determine his endgame.

"His goons are arriving daily, shadowing me while I perform my Sons of Liberty's duties. They haven't gone anywhere I hadn't allowed, but I need to know if their directives come from Sharpe alone. Or if the orders have come from the group's main benefactor."

"Ah," MJ said and then needed to clarify, "You think they are questioning your loyalty?"

"I'm getting closer to the wizard behind the curtain. They could be making sure I am who I say I am. Or to check that I am following their directives. Who knows...?" Mr. Black leaned forward in the chair and allowed the lamp's nearby glow to illuminate his face.

The light cast shadowing reliefs upon his angular cheekbones, making him look like the perfect villainous character. The rest of his appearance only magnified that persona.

Which MJ suspected Black intensely played upon to his advantage.

With the dark, ink-black hair styled short, framing close around his diamond-shaped face, the icy blue-grey of his eyes dominated his other features. Those chilling orbs pierced one's gaze with a coldness that deterred anyone from diving deeper into their depths.

MJ knew of only two people whom this man's looks and temperament didn't intimate. And again, he wasn't one of them.

Black shrugged and rested the underside of his forearms on his thighs. "Maybe I'm just being paranoid."

In this line of business, paranoia became commonplace. Also smart.

Their Commander-in-Chief excelled in both categories, allowing him to remain a couple of moves ahead of their opponents.

"But I believe Sharpe is making his move without orders from our target on both myself and William Maxwell. We need to be ready on both fronts. The Maxwell's' or-" Mr. Black adjusted the lapel of his jacket and smoothed the fabric along his chest before continuing, "Any of his associates are not to be harmed."

He got straight to the point by allowing his upper body to come closer to one of his top agents. "I need you and Michael to work together to find out what Sharpe's men are up to."

This, of course, made MJ sigh heavily. "Really? You want me and him to work together?" The majority of MJ's bulk shifted uncomfortably on the bed. And not because of any of his healing wounds. The idea of working closely with Black's shadow caused most of the tension to vibrate through his body.

Black waited a few seconds before adding fuel to the fire. "He suggested that you would be useful to him." He tilted his head to the side and gave MJ a searching look. "You prefer being cooped up here, in hiding?"

"You know I hate being sidelined," MJ practically hissed the words. "And I find it very unlikely he... even uttered my name as a possible partner. So, I know you must be in dire straits to put us together."

The boss abruptly sat up and rose from his chair. The sphere of light around the lamp was weak, so his upper body fell within the heavy darkness, concealing him from MJ's view.

When Black spoke, the sound of his voice seemed detached from his nearby form and embodied within the room's shadows. "Whether or not I'm in dire straits... is yet to be seen. However, it is well past time for you both to resolve your differences and learn to work together."

Black, used to stepping carefully over any terrain and not making a sound, made his way to the door in his usual fashion.

However, MJ, quite capable of discerning various sounds and locating their sources, knew his boss had moved away even without the aid of proper lighting. He waited, knowing a parting shot usually followed next.

"MJ, you are to remain dead to any other associates. Understood?"

"Yup," MJ replied, standing beside his bed, carefully stretching. He had to get back into fighting shape, which meant hours in front of a punching bag. His gaze went to his cell phone and ear pods. Many playlists were ready and waiting to be activated within arm's reach. And those heavy-metal genres would provide the edgy, raw energy needed to kick the shit out of whatever equipment Black had in the training area down in this hidden lair.

A grin flashed across his face when thinking of a good motivation image to tape on the outer leather for a productive outcome.

So intent on what came next, MJ assumed Black had given his final directive and had moved on, but the seemingly casual voice coming from the doorway did make him jolt in surprise.

"Oh, I made sure you had wheels to replace your Tahoe. You won't be disappointed. Michael parked it down the block. I also had him find you a new place to stay. This one has too many eyes on it to be helpful to you.

"I had Michael leave the coordinates in the GPS listing. Under... New River."

"Ha ha ha, real funny," Miles muttered with that meaningful reference. The New River gorge in West Virginia was where Sharpe dumped Miles Jennings's body to die.

But when a soft, barely-there sound reached MJ's ears, just outside his room, any other thoughts on Sharpe escaped him. It became hard to fathom that his ears heard correctly. Because Black making a joke was one thing, but that disturbing sound became something else entirely.

Did Black just chuckle, too?

Chapter Twenty-Five

Fifteen minutes later, Allison sat in the backseat of another dark grey Bronco with tinted windows. She bitterly wondered if Will's company bought them in bulk.

Sara sat beside her mother in a new child seat with the price tag still attached. The view outside the window kept a small child content enough as long as her small hand kept tethered to her mother's. Her unusual quietness began as soon as they entered the vehicle's interior.

It wasn't fear that held her tongue either. She practically vibrated with curiosity.

But whatever held the child's multitude of questions and comments, Allison was grateful. She couldn't handle answering anything her daughter could come up with at the moment.

Allison took the time to lean back and close her eyes.

As promised, the wedding happened speedily in her family's hotel room. Because of Will's connections, a judge had performed the deed.

She and Peggy had to explain Will's actions to Sara as best as they could. For Sara, Allison was already one of her Moms. But her reaction to Will being her real Daddy took everyone by surprise.

The acceptance of this news was as if the young child knew all along–and delighted in–that today became the day it got rectified. Sara squealed in delight when Will swooped her up in his arms and hurried to depart when the judge completed the wedding.

Allison thought Will was clueless about the small reprieve they received. Instead, she believed that confusion and anger would make way for tantrums and tears when Sara wanted to go back to the haven of the everyday routine and found that impossible.

A surge of helplessness rose inside. She shifted her attention downward and studied the simple gold band around her ring finger. The freehand resting on her lap closed in a tight fist. Her eyelids squeezed close.

It seemed to Allison that twenty-four hours had come and gone when, in reality, just a few hours had passed.

When her eyes opened, she immediately contacted Will in the rearview mirror.

Twisting away, she concentrated on the moving scenery out the window. The lights of traffic and store signs began morphing into blurry, misty, abstract shapes. A trembling hand impatiently brushed off the wetness running down both sides of her face.

Allison hated crying.

After all, a bitter thought arose: *What good does it do?*

Assuming by the cold FBI business approach, Will would never forgive her. But his high-handedness and possessive declaration about belonging to him had her so confused.

Is this just the physical attraction talking? Allison wondered if magnetism would be enough for their marriage. *And if what they did could be called a marriage.*

Regardless of what to call it, this new development put two new people in the crosshairs of Allison's family curse. Anyone with an affectionate association with the Buchanan family paid the ultimate price.

Death.

Her uncle had handled the constant threat by establishing tight control over everything in Allison's upbringing. Swarms of bodyguards, excessive training, limited freedom, and chilling displays of emotion served as his modus operandi.

But Allison hadn't wanted to be like that.

Instead, she found ways of staying on the peripheral edge of all those who had engaged her affection. Anyone looking at her from a distance would only see a friendly, bubbly facade she kept firmly in place.

Never did she reveal more than what one did to maintain a casual acquaintance.

And all of that had worked until her dealings with Will.

He had a knack for getting her shields to lower.

It took a moment to realize that they had stopped. She angled her head toward the door, wiping away the telling streaks on her cheeks. Through the spiraling turmoil, she remained unaware of Will's studying gaze throughout the ride to the airport.

Or the thoughts he picked up in her mind.

Sara's door opened, and Jeff leaned inside to undo the child's seatbelt.

Allison was undoing her own when she heard Will tell Jeff to take Sara on the plane.

Swiftly dipping down to look through the doors, the small private airplane parked outside surrounded by blinking ground lights came into view.

Her mouth opened several times, but words couldn't get past a suddenly dry throat. Pure pulsing fear washed over her. She had lost count of how many times her heart rate accelerated today.

Only with Will's arrival–at the door opening, blocking the view of the aircraft–did a sound escape. An anguished sob could be heard as he made his way into the back seat.

"Oh, God, I'm definitely tempting fate today." Allison's fear-glazed eyes pleaded into his. "Our baby..." She took several calming breaths that didn't do anything to lessen the fear.

"Relax, Allison–no. No, don't get out. Let me talk to you for a minute." As her body stilled, suddenly stiff with tension, he added, "Sweetheart, it's the only way."

"If I can have a minute to-" She held her fingers to her lips, preventing the sob from escaping. It broke free anyway.

Her hand violently shook.

Will would carry that expression with him to the grave, knowing he caused it. "Listen. Listen, Allison. You can't let Sara see you like this-"

"Don't you think I know that already? I'm trying to get it together." A hint of a rosy pink replaced her deadly pale pallor.

"I can sedate you. Would that help?" Will suggested.

"Don't tempt me. But Sara deserves to have me sitting next to her." She refocused back on her breathing technique. However, this time, it was more like double time. "I can do this!"

Allison was damn close to hyperventilating.

"Okay–fine. You win," Will quickly relinquished. "But first, can you lean forward and get my briefcase upfront?"

Happy for any distraction, Allison bent over the center console, looking for the briefcase. She couldn't see it anywhere.

Will hurriedly reached into his jacket pocket, took the lid off the syringe, and pierced through the pants' fabric into her rear end. When she squealed and tried to swing around, he held her in place and pressed down on the thumb to get the liquid out of the needle.

"I'm sorry. Damn, Ally, I'm so sorry. You'll be okay. I swear it." Will continued murmuring reassurances as he carefully eased her around so they faced each other. He softly brushed aside the tears streaking down her face.

"That hurt," she whimpered.

"And Baby, I'm sorry for that. But we need to get going."

Allison began to climb over him to get out of the car.

"Wait; let me go ahead of you." Will eased out and leaned inside the car's interior. He held onto an arm, guiding her out. "That's right, step down. I got you.

"Are you okay?"

Allison slowly nodded. "I don't want to be afraid of planes."

"I know, Baby, I know."

When her knees suddenly buckled with the effect of the drug coursing through the bloodstream, Will swung her up into his arms.

Her head rested perfectly in the nook of his neck.

She bit her lower lip, stealing a glimpse of the plane. "Will?" Allison whispered. A hard swallow moved down her throat before she added, "I think Jonathon's plane is bigger."

Will chuckled despite the recent events. "Well, we can't have that; I'll buy a bigger one when we get back." He angled his head back slightly. Watching Allison fight the drug's effect, he coaxed, "Go to sleep. You'll be fine. I promise."

Her heavy eyelids wanted to close, but fighting against it, she kept them open. She looked straight at him with eyes swimming in tears. "How can you promise that?" she demanded in a drug-induced state.

He grinned and announced, "I'm the pilot."

"Of course, you are," she mumbled before sleep overtook her.

Within moments, they reached the top of the small steps leading to the door opening. When Jeff motioned to take Allison from him, Will shook his head from side to side. In a primal, gut reaction, he held her tighter.

Jeff backed away and gestured for him to proceed ahead.

Tucked into one of the reclining seats, Sara was unsurprised by seeing her dad holding an unconscious Allison. "Auntie–Mommy, sleeping?" she asked, but her eye danced away to take in all the surrounding, more exciting things.

Will reaffirmed their earlier talk, "Yes, Mommy's sleeping. She won't wake up until tomorrow. Flying isn't her thing. Let me go tuck her in, and then we can be on our way."

Sara's hands clapped excitedly in the seat.

Having heard so much about riding on a plane from her best friend, Linda Kimble, she was eager to experience her own adventure. Her young eyes ignored the plush, expensive decor to view the action beyond the windows. Large, moving equipment, rushed personnel finishing up their orders, and other parked planes nearby served far more incredible sights to be seen.

Linda had gone to Disney with family too, but they got to fly in a plane instead of driving the whole way, like Sara's family.

"Oh yes, yes, yes!" she happily chanted.

"Okay then," Will replied while shifting around in time to catch Jeff's amused expression. "Can you get Sara settled in while I lay Allison down in the back bedroom?"

With hands tucked in his pockets, Jeff nodded once. Their gazes locked.

An unspoken message passed between them. No telepathy was required before Will swung back, heading toward the back of the aircraft. Sparing his partner a glance, the determined strides and regal bearing of Will's body language as he walked away told Jeff everything.

A king was staking his claim and preparing for battle.

To keep.

To protect.

"Come on, kiddo," Jeff teased Sara as he undid the seat buckle. "Let's go check out the cockpit real quick."

Sara spun back to watch Allison being carried away.

Jeff, noticing the hesitation, said, "You know..." His voice sounded casual and coaxing. "We should get pictures of you sitting in the co-captain's chair. That way, you can tell your Mom all about it tomorrow morning." He watched in satisfaction as Sara whirled around and shot Jeff a huge smile.

"Can we?

"Did you bring a camera?

"Oh boy, wait until Auntie- I mean, Mommy and Linda see them." Entering the cockpit, she leaned back and tilted her petite head up at him. "Can you take a few of me in that chair?" Pointing to the pilot's seat, she implored with pleading eyes.

Recognizing Allison's features in Sara's miniature version, Jeff's usual cocky grin spread across his face. "Copy, captain, I'll take plenty."

Sara squirmed with childish delight while her hands clapped even more. In a flash, she demanded to be picked up so that kisses and hugs were gifted with child-like enthusiasm.

He chuckled and playfully tossed her up in the air after returning the fluttering kisses. Sara's exuberant and excited squeals filled the plane.

Will had entered the small bedroom when he heard his daughter's laughter. His hold on Allison tightened. Heading toward the double bed positioned in the center of the room, his pace slowed before coming to a stop.

The bedspread and covers laid pulled back. Their color and thread count were dismissed, with his thoughts running amok. But those pressing matters skirted to the side as he gently lowered her down. And his focus sharpened on one concern, catching that distressed murmur escape from her parted lips.

He moved slightly away. With his legs losing strength, he slowly sank down on the edge of the bed. Lowering his head into open hands, he slowly unraveled the tightly coiled panic that had a tight fist around his heart.

Admitting finally, the fear of losing Allison had been ahead of everything else. Even having been wrung out over the child's discovery, faded in comparison.

However, the terrorist organization's continuing attacks did come a close second. But that had more to do with that problem's effect on his new family.

Will prayed they remained in the dark concerning Sara as much as he had been.

Chapter Twenty-Six

Allison," a recognizable voice called to her, pulling her from the deepest level of sleep.

Her eyes blinked open. When she found herself in a hospital bed, a marring frown appeared on her face. The room seemed familiar.

"Allison," the voice called to her again.

She rose on her elbows, darting a gaze around the room. Most of its perimeter stayed in blurry, indistinct shapes and shadows, like looking through a shard of tinted glass.

Before fear could take hold, her legal guardian stepped from the darker shadows into the surrounding light by the bed. "Uncle?" she whispered.

What is going on? Again, she glanced at the space, catching the details she had missed earlier. A memory clicked in place.

The familiarity now made sense. This was the room Allison had awoken from back in college after the airplane accident.

Her uncle stood before her again, just like the last time.

A dream.

Senator Buchanan sat beside her, unlike that other time when he stood before her in a rigid stance that matched his temperament. He patted her leg softly, soothing her, as she stayed frozen in confusion.

"You remember what I spoke of that day?" he asked, stroking her in small circular pats on her leg, just above her ankle.

"I told you the 'Buchanan Curse' hurts many people close to us. Like your mother and stepfather. Like your father, my brother, end up sacrificing their lives because of that curse."

"Yes. I remember," she said, pulling away from his comforting touch as she sat straighter in the bed. "I've spent most of my adult life protecting others from it. My daughter, my sister, Jake, Debbie, even you." Allison's voice dropped lower when she continued, "Ah, even Will."

"I know," he replied, pulling his hand back and resting it on his upper thigh. "You broke it off with him because things became serious. You got scared. And I blamed myself for the fear I built up in your mind." Easing off the bed, he stood and came closer to her. "I was wrong to do that to you, Allison.

"And you could also place the whole mess with Mark on my shoulders. I shouldn't have pushed for the marriage. But I thought he was a safe choice for you." He sighed heavily, and his chin fell to his chest.

"He didn't do right by you and only wanted one thing from your union," he divulged. His tone was clipped, angry.

"I know. He wanted what my family's connection could bring him," she admitted softly.

"No, he wanted a child from you," he corrected.

She tilted her head to the side, and her gaze turned unfocused. Her first marriage, although short, still left a scar. Knowing their union wasn't a love match didn't remove the sting of rejection.

But realizing she had been played in more ways than one stung even more.

"It's true." Her uncle interrupted the dark thoughts spiraling through her mind. Her attention pulled back toward him as his explanation continued, "Once I knew what he planned, I took matters into hand," he confessed.

"The doctor's prescriptions," she added.

He nodded and patted her thigh a few times before shifting away.

A short span of silence stood between them. But Allison didn't sense an emotional void like some of their past talks. She felt a warmth, remaining steady and present, anchoring their connection.

When turning back, his gaze rose and locked onto hers. A shrug lifted his shoulders before he added, "As well as other things you don't need to know about today. But I promise to tell you soon.

"Right now, your attention should stay focused on Will." His grey-blue eyes glinted with an intensity that seemed to heat the air around them. "You two belong together."

Allison adamantly shook her head from side to side. "No, I won't let you use Will's power for-" Senator Buchanan's hearty laugh shocked her into silence. She hadn't heard that sound in such a long time.

"I don't have designs on Will's gift, Allison. My only concern is keeping you and Sara safe. Will can do that far better than I."

"Still..." Allison sighed, slumping her shoulders in defeat. "It's best to keep my distance. He could be-"

"Hurt?" her uncle interrupted. "We all can be hurt, honey. And death waits for no one. Withstanding our family curse or not. Life isn't safe, with no guarantees.

"Trials are a part of living, child. Keeping people away to protect them leaves you without the support to navigate those trials." Squatting down to allow his gaze to stay level with hers, he added, "and others without yours."

Allison looked away. Her hands, resting on her lap, clenched in fists. To outright dismiss his advice bubbled to the surface. Changing now was daunting. How would she even begin to rectify?

Look at what hung between Will and herself because of her choices.

Is forgiveness possible for keeping Sara a secret for so long?

Pushing Will away and hiding Sara under everyone's noses did accomplish something. Her sister, Bob, Jake, and Debbie, benefited too from her friendly but guarded relationships. Weren't they all safe because of those precautions?

Allison released a shaky breath, pressing the layer of soft cotton with the palm of her hand and straightening out the wrinkles. The toll for keeping people at a distance was already paid. Damages have occurred, forming emotional chasms. Too many to count.

And Allison's childhood, natural disposition, repressed for so long, struggled with handling personal interactions any differently. What would that even look like?

How could she freely express affection for her family, friends, and Will?

Would it come off as sincere? Or seem unnatural and practiced?

She shook her head from side to side, groaning silently in dismay. *Is this the right thing to do, or is it just wishful thinking? A dream?*

"This is a dream, niece," Senator Buchanan assured her, patting her knee. "But, also real. Something is growing stronger, needing to come out, and I thought it prudent to reveal myself to you like this."

"You can travel in dreams?" she whispered in awe.

He grinned before replying, "Pretty cool, hey?"

She shrugged in an offhanded casualness that her uncle could see through. He knew how much she struggled with normalcy regarding others with power, seeing herself as weak.

But he knew better. His frame shifted, further straightening his posture. "Trials are coming, Allison. Ones I can't protect you from."

"What trails?" she huffed. "What aren't you telling me?"

"A lot, I'm afraid. But for now, leaving you in the dark is safer. If I tell you, it may alter events that need to take place. Unfortunately, that brings the danger closer, and I can't be there for you." His voice held an insistence. A pulsing emotion came through their connection, and her heart rate accelerated.

"Caution is prudent," he softly encouraged. His voice grew louder, continuing, "But avoidance is cowardice when taken too far."

He let go and stood before her. "Don't make the same mistakes I did, love. Learn to protect them instead of pushing them away until it is too late.

"Allies are essential to withstand what is coming. That will only happen if you allow the bonds to lock-" He emphasized his point by grasping her hand and holding it tight. "That takes interaction, physical and emotional connections."

He tugged on her hand. "Do you understand what I'm telling you?"

She nodded back as her hand clasped his. "I think so, Uncle. I'll..." She puffed out a loud exhale, squeezing his hand tighter. "I will try."

"Good, honey. Now, get some rest. Things are about to get interesting," he said before fading away.

"Uncle!" she cried, looking around the empty room. She didn't want to lose that connection with him and her affection toward him and from him. The remembering of what they had so long ago swept into her thoughts.

Flooded into her heart.

That protective shield, held in place for so long, cracked. A slight pang of pain took her breath away. Her hand pressed the area on her chest, and that ache lingered.

She tried to wake up, stressing about what changes her uncle suggested, but everything began fading as a deeper sleep pulled her back under.

****

Will's head rose, tilting in speculation. Allison's soft plea and fretful shifting caught his gaze. A heavy sigh escaped him when nothing else followed, and she settled back into a restful pose. His fingers combed through a head of hair, pulling and tugging at several tangles. He welcomed the pain, needing the distraction of wayward thoughts.

Sara's laughter carried across the length of the plane to him; swiftly dropping his hands down, they gripped his knees.

Other pressing thoughts rushed to the surface.

A strong suspicion that Sara's true parentage hadn't as easily fooled Allison's uncle as it did him. And some of Senator Buchanan's cryptic comments in the past now made perfect sense.

But figuring out all the why's and what's would have to wait.

Will shifted around, tucking the covers tight to his bride's slim figure. He hesitated, keeping a fixed gaze on her reposed form while warring thoughts fought for a foothold.

How did they know about our arrival at the airport and the hotel?

Has any information come up on the man Jeff left alive? Or my traitorous employees?

Who else in my company is working for the enemy?

Is the safe house compromised, too?

At this very moment, the heads of numerous state and federal divisions were formulating options. Frank Marshall would want to speak with him, and they would argue about Will's role in this investigation.

Will would refuse to stay on the sidelines anymore.

I want the threat eliminated. This steely resolve burned through all the other conflicting thoughts battling for attention.

He stood up and headed out of the cabin. His gait became sure and smooth. The eyes glinted with a fierceness that promised retribution for anyone foolish enough to get in his way.

They needed to get back to West Virginia. Then, he'd find a way to keep his new family safe from this terrorist organization.

After that, Will had to convince his reluctant client to stay his bride.

Because no way in Hell would he allow Allison's childhood fear of **'The Buchanan's Curse'** to keep them apart.

The End

Guardians, Inc. Series- Part 1

Excerpt of Waffling Bride

Book 2 in the Guardians, Inc. series

Allison tried pulling away. "Did you actually have me handcuffed?"

A lot of shit went down yesterday.

He spread his arms out above his head and flexed into a slow stretch.

But two amazing things also came out of it. One had been his daughter, Sara.

With his FBI partner and best friend's help, Jeffery Collins handled Sara like a pro when she had fallen asleep on the plane long before they landed. As Will had hoped, she remained deeply asleep–like most three-year-olds–when carried to the room across from them.

Will and Jeff felt equally driven to the task, firmly readjusted their priorities. After getting Allison settled into her room, Will met up with his partner, and they got to work.

Kicking up some metaphorical stones in the investigation, they had to address the complications of their enemy's recent attacks. As of last night, Florida's office hadn't gotten anything from the one that survived. But Jeff had remained hopeful something would give from their phones.

A glance at Will's custom watch laying on the bedside table confirmed they slept in late. The fact he had been able to sleep at all surprised the hell out of him. But then, after tossing and turning for an hour or so in a bed down the hall, the decision became obvious.

Why not just go to the source of my problems?

Which, of course, proved right. Only after lying beside Allison, listening to her relaxed breathing, did Will finally recognize the other amazing gift.

But wanting to talk to Allison first thing this morning, he did this one thing before submitting to sleep. And he truly had used the cuffs mainly so that she couldn't avoid him. Although, having her annoyed would give him some satisfaction as well.

She put him through hell yesterday.

Presently, that woman looked like she'd take a swing at him to accompany that fiery glare. Although, it lost some of its impact when only one of her witch-hazel eyes–now a deep, forest-green–could be viewed. The rest of her face remained obscurely hidden behind the wavy, disarray of hair surrounding her slim oval-shaped face.

But what could be seen still successfully translated the flash of ire as her one arm–linked with his–had to tag along with his stretching movements.

Adding insult to injury, her petite frame had to accommodate his much larger one. But she made use of her free hand to swipe away the tumbled long, silky, dark-chestnut tresses from her face. All the more able, a full-frontal assault of flashing eyes, naturally pink, full-shaped lips, and flushed colored cheeks got sent his way.

Who could sympathize when the end result provided this visual reaction?

Definitely not Will. Taking his sweet time finding the key, he unlocked his and her wrist and grinned at her outraged face. His positive frame of mind had more to do with his resolved feelings for Allison than catching up on sleep. He leaned in closer and gave her a quick kiss on the lips.

"How did you sleep?" He quickly put on his wrist device now that the cuffs were off.

Allison sputtered. Finding him bare-chested, unshaven, and looking incredibly sexy in her bed was one thing. But his gorgeous body stretched out and on display, while grinning and kissing her became something else entirely.

Will's expression remained openly cheerful as he pushed her back down while stretching out on his side. Inclining over her, moving his one, unclothed, muscular leg, he successfully pinned her in place. "Now, let's just relax, Allison," he coaxed.

Too unsettled to provide better mental shields, Allison practically shouted through their telepathic link. Yeah, right, like that's going to happen, she scoffed at him.

"Yes, it can," Will promised. "We need to get a few things straight. Mmm?"

His exhaled breath tickled her left ear, as he got even closer. *He is too much!*

"Yes, I am," Will replied back to her inner thoughts. He slowly shifted his tactile exploration down toward Allison's neck. Anticipation had him grinning when her head whipped around to block his wandering lips. He got just what he wanted.

"Are you comfortable, Ally?" he whispered close to her ear.

To have faced him head-on became a big mistake. She found her breathing becoming irregular. Her flushed face and eyes expressed numerous emotions, rebellion, confusion, and longing. But she willed herself to be unaffected.

He forced a slight chuckle. Allison's nearness also began clouding his focus. His leg slowly moved away, making sure his movement caressed against her bare skin. His slow retreat provided a direct attack on her senses.

Allison's eyes narrowed to a stern glare.

But Will could feel her trembling. And a vulnerability flickered across her beautiful face.

"Is this your revenge, Will? Using this attraction against me?"

"Revenge? Isn't that a little dramatic?" Will tilted his head to the side with glittering specks highlighted in his golden-brown eyes. "But I guess leaving a federal officer stranded in that diner's parking lot. To run from my protection and fly petrified across the country. Not to mention, keeping a three-year secret could be due to a dramatic flair."

"What?" she hesitated. Confused. By all accounts, Will deserved to be mad. Instead, he looked relaxed and sounded playful.

When she stayed tongue-tied, he advanced, "Have you developed a dramatic flair since we stopped being lovers?"

Wetting her lips with her tongue, she regretted it when it drew Will's attention. "Umm…" A voice, barely-there as her gaze got drawn to Will's lips too.

Will's eyes remained glued to her mouth. He leaned in closer until his lips just barely touched hers. "Let's get an answer, another way."

Their kiss instantly swept them both over. Jeff would have a surfing term to name the occurrence, but Will didn't care at the moment.

Allison went willingly into the madness falling into the long spiral ride of pleasurable sensations and the eruption of heat. Will had always had the power to shut off her mind and make her want oblivion. She pulled him closer, craving the weight of him.

Caught in a trap of his own making, Will had no inclination to pull free. Their mutual attraction provided such intense pleasures. He reminded her how good they were together with loving touches and teasing strokes.

For many moments the sounds of their mutual passion filled the room before Will fought to get control of his desires. Her smell. Her skin. Her touch. Drove him on. Within the vortex of fast-beating hearts, dizzying pleasures, and unrelenting lustful cravings, he wanted–no, needed–it to be her decision. Not his coercion.

It took tremendous effort to soften his kisses. Whispering loving promises, he slowly pulled them back from the brink. He had too much riding on this.

Sex was just sex if the commitment was left out. He wanted to commit the shit out of what he and Allison had. And what they had wasn't just a physical connection. He understood that now.

But their union would not be consummated this morning.

www.ingramcontent.com/pod-product-compliance
Lightning Source LLC
Chambersburg PA
CBHW052356030726
47599CB00014B/1085